Christmas at Cartwright Manor

SEASONS *of* LITTLETON 2

Christmas at Cartwright Manor

SHAELA KAY

 Blue Water Books

Other books in this series

Christmas at Edgewood Park

Published by Blue Water Books
Richland, WA

Cover photo © JuliaSha/Depositphotos.com

© 2018 Shaela Kay Odd
Visit the author at www.shaelakay.com

This book is a work of fiction. While great care has been taken to ensure historical accuracy of dates and locations, characters and events in this book are products of the author's imagination and are represented fictitiously. Any likeness to any person, living or dead, is purely coincidental.

*For every woman who has ever
longed to be a mother*

Chapter 1

December 1851
Littleton, Norfolk, England

Eleanor snuggled the chubby infant in her arms, brushing away a lock of chestnut curls to place an affectionate kiss on her forehead. Cecelia's eyelids fluttered but she did not wake. Slowly, Eleanor drifted back into the parlor, where Albert was standing next to the fire. He looked up at her approach.

"Is she asleep?" he asked hesitantly.

"Yes," Eleanor replied, smiling at him. Albert's face relaxed.

"You have such a way with her," he said.

Eleanor looked down at the babe in her arms, love blossoming in her breast. Cecelia's lips were gently parted in sleep, and one little fist clung tightly to a piece of ribbon adorning Eleanor's dress. Eleanor slowly pulled it from her grasp.

"Oh, thank heavens!"

The Cartwrights turned as Eleanor's younger brother, Nathaniel, stepped into the room. "Bless you, Nora, for getting her to sleep. I've given up on Michael," he sighed. "Beatrice is with him now, trying to convince him that his new toys will be waiting for him in the morning. She will be relieved to see that you've managed to get Cece to sleep, at least."

"It *has* been quite a busy day for them," Albert said.

"It has been a wonderful day!" Eleanor said, kissing Cecelia's little fist. "Cece's first Christmas will surely be one to remember."

"*You* certainly remembered," Nathaniel said dryly. "Really, I do not believe we shall have to purchase Cece clothes, toys, or blankets for at least a decade, after the entourage of gifts you brought for her. Nor for Michael, I daresay."

"An aunt has every right to dote on her niece and nephew," Eleanor said airily, swaying gently to keep Cecelia slumbering.

"I shall not argue with you, then," Nathaniel replied. "I learned as a boy it was quite a fruitless endeavor."

He slumped into a chair and closed his eyes, clearly exhausted. Eleanor turned her attention back to her niece, singing softly to her. Albert walked over to stand beside her. "Eleanor," he murmured, "I wonder if–"

"Shh," Eleanor said, looking up with a slight frown. "You might wake her."

Albert's solemn blue eyes were no longer smiling.

"We shall be on our way soon. Then we can talk," she said. Eleanor smiled tightly, tipping her chin up to be kissed. Albert bent and brushed his lips softly against her own, the scar across his face making his pucker uneven.

2

"Thank you, Mrs. Cartwright," he said.

"You are most welcome, Mr. Cartwright."

Albert and Eleanor had been married for nine years, but the lapse of nearly a decade had not diminished their love for one another at all. The burst of love and affection which had ignited their courtship had settled into a comfortable, steadfast warmth—in much the same way as a match ignites the kindling which grows into a steady fire.

Ten minutes later, Beatrice Eves walked into the room. "Oh, Nora!" she said, a tired smile on her face. "Thank you so much for helping with Cece. I can take her now."

"I do not mind holding her," Eleanor replied, but Beatrice was already easing the sleeping infant from her arms.

"Thank you," she said, "but she will sleep better in her crib."

Cradling her sleeping daughter, Beatrice walked past her weary husband, whom she gently nudged.

"Nathan! What an atrocious host you are, sleeping in front of our guests," she chided him. He groaned and sat up.

"Since when must I regard my sister as a guest?" he grumbled. Albert chuckled.

"We should be going. It has been a long day for everyone," Albert said, looking at his wife. Eleanor nodded.

"Let me put Cece down, and then we shall see you off," Beatrice said.

The carriage was waiting when she returned from the nursery. Eleanor tied her new bonnet under her chin, encasing her dark hair in its velvet embrace. She was tall and willowy, but her husband, Albert, stood nearly a head taller. He helped Eleanor on with her cloak, then took his walking stick in hand as they stepped into the chill December night. Eleanor glanced back at her brother as Albert handed her into the carriage. He was standing in the doorway with his arm around his wife, whose head rested on his shoulder. It was clear from their looks that they were tired but content, and Eleanor turned away, blinking back tears as the carriage lurched forward.

The night was dark, but a thin, silver moon shone bravely down on the snowy landscape. Pinpricks of light in the inky sky flashed and winked as they rode through the woods, heading towards the glow which marked their home at Cartwright Manor. Eleanor watched as the house grew larger the closer they drew, the pain in her heart growing with every turn of the wheels.

When they at last pulled up to the front doors, Eleanor could hardly keep her tears in check. Albert helped her out of the carriage, his sympathetic smile pinching her heart and causing a few tears to run down her cheeks. She brushed them hastily aside.

The entrance hall was dark, lit only by two candelabras on either side of the massive front doors and a pair of candlesticks on the center table. Most of the staff were celebrating the holiday with their own families, and the manor was cold and lonely without their usual presence. Eleanor pulled off her hat and gloves, setting them on the table.

"Nora?"

She paused as Albert said her name, biting her lip. He set his hat and cane on the table, and then he was there, wrapping her in his arms. She no longer had the strength to hold back her tears; they poured from her eyes, leaving tracks upon her cheeks that glistened in the candlelight.

"It is so hard, Albert," she whispered.

"I know, my dear, I know."

Her body shook, and she buried her face in his shoulder. After a few minutes, her sobs subsided, and she pulled away to retrieve her handkerchief. Albert kept his arms around her.

"It does not seem fair," she said, her words muffled. "So many poor families have more mouths to feed than they can possibly afford, and yet," she gestured to the room around them, which was so large the candlelight did not even reach the far walls, "we have more than enough to provide for a dozen children, and still our home is empty."

"It is *not* empty," Albert said with feeling. "It was empty before you came into my life, but now it is full of love. Your love. Our love."

She smiled at him—a weak, tolerant smile—then reached a hand up to stroke his cheek. Her fingers slid over the scar which stretched from his left temple to below his chin. He pressed his hand over hers, holding it to his face.

"I love you, Eleanor," he said, his voice gentle. "I wish I could take this pain from you."

Fresh tears welled up in her eyes, and she collapsed against his chest, sobbing. Albert held her, as he had countless times before, waiting for the flood to cease.

It was a very long time before it did.

Chapter 2

The year 1851 went out as quietly as a lamp, and the new year came in just as softly. The few weeks following the Christmas holidays were quiet and calm, with only a few small flurries of snow to cover the damp, muddy ground. If Mr. Eves had still been alive, he would have spent the time reminiscing of past Christmas holidays, and insisting that the most recent celebration had been the best one yet. But Eleanor's father had passed away six years ago, and no one else bothered to remember now.

It used to follow that Eleanor felt happily exhausted at this time of year, after having spent all her time and energy ensuring that her friends and neighbors in Littleton had a happy and blessed holiday season. That was before her illness, when she was still managing the bazaar. A few years back, shortly after Nathaniel and Beatrice married, scarlet fever had swept through the community and Eleanor was stricken ill, having contracted the disease while caring for those already afflicted. Her new sister-in-law, anxious to establish herself within the neighborhood, stepped in to run the bazaar in her place that year. Beatrice did such a marvelous job, and the townspeople spoke so highly of her, that Eleanor had not had the heart to reclaim it. Now, with the bazaar and holidays well and over, instead of feeling tired, Eleanor felt restless. The whole of January and February stretched before her—empty, cold, barren.

Wrapping her arms around herself, Eleanor went in search of the housekeeper, whom she discovered in one of the drawing rooms.

"Mrs. Winthrop, I wonder if there is anything I can help you with this morning," she said.

The matronly housekeeper smiled indulgently at her. "Now, mistress, you know very well I have everything under control. There's not a thing you can do for me, but is there something I can do for you? A bit of tea and cake, perhaps? You look tired; you should rest."

Eleanor shook her head. "No, thank you. I just want to feel useful."

"Useful! Dearie, you are one of the most useful creatures I know. Go put your feet up; I'll send Mary along with some refreshment."

Sighing, Eleanor was shooed from the room by the kindly woman, but instead of heading upstairs to her sitting room, she turned down the long, narrow hallway leading to the back of the house. Cold stone walls pressed in on her, and she held her breath, quickening her pace until the hall opened again. Three steps led down into the spacious kitchen area, which was bustling with activity.

"Good morning, mistress," one of the maids said, bobbing a curtsy.

"Good morning, Fanny." The yeasty smell of fresh-baked bread filled Eleanor's nostrils, and she smiled. "Do you need any help down here?"

"Laws, no!" Mrs. Reuben, the head cook interjected. "You get yourself back upstairs this instant, Mrs. Cartwright. I have plenty of help and even if I didn't, do you think I'd let you soil your pretty hands? Laws, what is the world coming to? You've nothing to do down here. Get along with you."

"But–"

"Tsh! Get along with you, now, get along! Maggie, help Mrs. Cartwright to her room."

Eleanor sighed again and turned away. Though the fever had left her in a somewhat weakened state, she was by no means an invalid. She had only the occasional headache, and though she tired a bit more easily, the entire staff—and Albert, besides—treated her as if she were still at death's door.

Eleanor allowed herself to be escorted into the entrance hall, but would go no further. "I can manage the stairs myself," she said. "Thank you for your help, but please return to your duties. I will be all right."

Her servant bobbed a curtsy and turned back, while Eleanor continued upstairs alone, to the little parlor adjacent her bedroom. She entered the room just as another maid—sent by Mrs. Winthrop, no doubt—was setting down a tray of tea and biscuits.

"Good morning, mistress," the housemaid said. "I've brought some tea, and your letters. Will you be needing anything else?"

"No, thank you," Eleanor replied, too tired to object to the coddling again.

The girl curtsied and left the room, and Eleanor sat down, picking up the small stack of papers beside the tea service. The first was a note from Mrs. Lewis, the pastor's wife, inviting Eleanor to dine with her the following day. Eleanor smiled, grateful to her friend for reaching out. Mrs. Lewis knew how difficult this time of year now was for Eleanor, and never hesitated to offer a kind word or a shoulder to cry on.

The next piece of mail was a note from Beatrice, informing her sister-in-law that she was far too busy with the children to come for tea today, but that Eleanor was welcome to stop by for some refreshment if she so wished. Eleanor's throat tightened, and she hastily set the letter aside. How good it would feel, to be "far too busy" with such things!

Pushing the thought from her mind, Eleanor poured herself some tea and picked up a book, resigned once more to her empty house, her lonely room, and her own company.

The next day dawned clear and cold. Eleanor, anxious for her visit with Mrs. Lewis, made herself ready early in the morning. Though Mrs. Winthrop saw to the needs of the household, she wished to stop at the general store before her visit with the pastor's wife.

"Send the Lewises my regards," Albert called as she climbed into the carriage. Eleanor smiled and waved, anxious to be on her way.

Though the roads were mostly clear, it was a very bumpy ride into town. A light snow had fallen earlier in the week, concealing the deep, uneven ruts which had solidified into frozen mounds of mud. Eleanor was glad to finally alight from the carriage in front of Grantham's Mercantile.

The bell over the door jingled merrily as she stepped into the cozy room. Shelves and tables lined the walls, filled with various articles for home and farm. Eleanor breathed in the rich aroma of coffee grounds and wood smoke, looking around for any of her neighbors. Her countenance fell as she saw that the store was bereft of other customers.

"Ah, Mrs. Cartwright! How can I help you today?"

"How do you do, Mr. Grantham?" Eleanor said to the man behind the counter. He smiled at her, wiping the perspiration from his balding head with a checked handkerchief.

"Not one to complain," he said, "but 'tis a mite warm for me in here."

Eleanor smiled. "If you step outside for a moment, you might appreciate it more."

"Still cold, eh?"

"Bitterly," Eleanor replied, moving towards the counter. Her only reason for stopping at the store was to chat with her friends and neighbors, but since no one had gathered therein, she cast her mind upon something—anything—to give reason for her visit. "Have you any *congou* tea leaves on hand?" she asked.

"Hmm, not sure if I do. Wait a spell while I check the back—I haven't any up here."

Mr. Grantham disappeared down the hallway, and Eleanor walked slowly around the store, admiring the placement of merchandise and the variety of items available. A small basket full of ribbons caught her eye, and she stopped to examine them. Each ribbon was individually looped and tied in a neat little bundle, with a tiny bow made from the same ribbon to showcase each pattern and color. She picked one up, running her fingers along the smooth satin material.

"Mrs. Eves did that," Mr. Grantham said proudly, walking back into the room, "as well as the dried flower arrangements in the window." Eleanor looked to where he indicated. "She certainly has style, that sister of yours."

"Yes, she does."

"And what an event she put on for us, eh? The church looked like a right cathedral by the time she was finished decorating for the bazaar. Made me right proud to be a part of it."

Eleanor forced herself to smile at the kindly gentleman, knowing he did not mean to offend. She reached for the bag of tea leaves he had placed on the counter.

"Thank you, Mr. Grantham. Might I have a pound of sugar as well, please?"

"Certainly. White or brown?"

"White, please."

She waited while he broke off the required amount from the tall cone of sugar. He weighed the pieces on a scale and wrapped them in paper for her. "Did you need anything else today?"

"No, thank you. But give my regards to Mrs. Grantham."

"I certainly will."

Eleanor escaped through the door she had so happily entered only minutes before. Glancing up the street, she could see several evergreen wreaths—the last remaining vestiges from the holiday bazaar—still hanging on door fronts and over windows. She sighed, turning to cross the street towards the church. She was happy to see that Mrs. Lewis, at least, had removed the offending garlands from the chapel doors.

The Lewises lived in a small house directly behind the church. Years ago a terrible storm had destroyed the old building, along with the attached apartment designated for the minister's family. As the wealthiest man in the neighborhood and newly-called philanthropist, Albert Cartwright had stepped in to rebuild the church, as well as a separate parsonage. Both new buildings were well-made and quite comfortable, and Mrs. Lewis was delighted with their new home.

Eleanor's knock was answered by the young woman Mrs. Lewis employed as a maid-of-all-work. The lass had more competence than complexion, but her smile was genuine as she greeted Eleanor and stepped back.

"Good day, Mrs. Cartwright," the maid said cheerfully. "Mrs. Lewis has been expecting you."

Eleanor thanked the girl and followed her into the parlor, where she found her friend bent over her needlework. The years had been kind to the minister's wife, and though the silver streaks in her auburn hair had multiplied, her face was still youthful. She was Eleanor's dearest friend, and the closest thing to a mother she had ever known. She smiled and stood as Eleanor was introduced.

"My dear, how glad I am to see you!"

"And I you, Mrs. Lewis. Thank you for inviting me."

The ladies embraced before taking their seats, and Mrs. Lewis poured out. She handed Eleanor a cup. "How are you?" she asked, raising her brow. Eleanor sighed.

"Feeling as useful as a watering pot in Noah's flood," she said. Her friend smiled sympathetically.

"Have you been feeling well?"

"My headaches are not as frequent, and I am no longer winded after my walks."

"That is good news."

"Yes, except that the entire household continues to treat me as if I were to collapse at any moment," Eleanor said, exasperated. "I cannot even go upstairs without someone wanting to send a servant with me."

"My dear, you can hardly blame them," Mrs. Lewis said gently. "You nearly slipped away from us, you know. Mr. Cartwright was simply beside himself."

"I know," Eleanor sighed, "but I am well now."

Eleanor did not want to talk of her health, and she turned the conversation to other things. Eventually they landed on the topic of fashion and the new style for wider skirts, which required hoops and crinolines to support them.

"Beatrice received a shipment of dresses and petticoats from London for Christmas," Eleanor said. "Some of the skirts are so wide, I do not know how she shall fit through the door!"

Mrs. Lewis laughed. "A gift from Nathaniel?"

Eleanor nodded.

"Your brother simply dotes on her."

"Yes, and she dotes on the children," Eleanor replied with a wistful smile.

Mrs. Lewis heard the longing in her voice. "Have you considered seeking the advice of another physician?" she asked gently.

Eleanor shook her head decidedly. "No. We have consulted with two already, and they both agree that there appears to be nothing the matter with me. I have no desire to be subjected to further examination."

There was a long pause, during which time Mrs. Lewis observed her friend carefully. Eleanor had grown thin—very thin—in recent years. Her rosy cheeks were now pale and hollow, and though she was no longer a young woman, she looked decidedly older than her thirty-nine years. Fine lines around her eyes and lips bore testament to the sorrow she had seen in recent years, and Mrs. Lewis reached out, laying a hand on her arm.

"I am sorry," she said.

Eleanor nodded her thanks. "Albert feels it, too. He shall never have a son. He shall never have an heir." She dropped her face into her hands. "Oh, how I wish it were not so!"

Mrs. Lewis rose from her chair and went to sit beside her on the sofa. After a few minutes Eleanor wiped her eyes and smiled weakly at her friend. Mrs. Lewis gave her a gentle squeeze.

"Eleanor, you are one of the kindest, bravest women I know," she said. "And though you may not leave a legacy for your own children, you have certainly left an impression upon the children of Littleton. Why, just look at Johnny Whitman!"

A hesitant smile crept onto Eleanor's face. "Johnny has grown into a fine young man," she said.

"He certainly has. He is a credit to his parents and the entire parish. And he owes much of it to Mr. Cartwright. And yourself."

The smile on her face melted away, and Eleanor looked down. "I have not done much for anyone, in quite some time," she said. "Not since before I was ill."

"My dear, everyone needs to be cared for at times. Even those who are used to caring for others."

"But what am I to do now? Albert does not need my care, I have no children of my own, and between yourself and my sister-in-law, there is not a family in town who wants for my help."

"It may appear that way," Mrs. Lewis mused, "but I have found that when it seems as though everyone's needs are met and there is nothing more for me to do, I am often looking at things from the wrong quarter."

She set her saucer on the table and folded her hands in her lap. "The Lord works in mysterious ways, Eleanor. Rest assured, your time will come again."

"And until then?"

Mrs. Lewis smiled brightly. "Enjoy the rest while you can. I do not think it will last long."

Eleanor sighed, and Mrs. Lewis poured her another cup of tea.

Chapter 3

The town of Littleton was no more than a single street with a handful of shops and houses standing alongside it. A blacksmith shop stood beside the livery stable, which was on the same side of the street as Grantham's Mercantile. The new church stood at the end of the lane, and aside from the big houses, it was the only building large enough to accommodate all of the town's residents, the majority of whom were tenant farmers. Woods and meadows hugged the town, their varied hues changing with the seasons year after year.

Since many of the town's occupants lived on isolated farms, Sunday services were as much about the socializing as they were about the sermon. The whole town turned out in their finest, to listen to Father Lewis preach from the gospels and hear the latest news from their neighbors. Eleanor sat beside Albert in the Cartwright pew, looking across at her brother's family, who sat on the same bench she had occupied with her father for most of her life. Beatrice was holding little Cece in her arms, while six-year-old Michael squirmed between his parents. He caught his aunt looking at him and grinned. Eleanor smiled back.

Mrs. Lewis sat alone in the small pew near the front, occasionally coughing into her handkerchief. Eleanor watched and listened to her throughout the sermon with growing alarm. When the congregation had sung the final hymn and the usual hum of conversation filled the room, she went straight to her friend's side.

"Are you unwell?" Eleanor asked, concern creasing her brow.

Mrs. Lewis waved her off.

"Just a little chest cold. The time of year, you know."

Eleanor nodded, looking around. Though most of the town was in attendance, a few families were absent. The Whitmans, with their four children, were not there, nor old Miss Anderson. Eleanor made a mental note to inquire after them in the morning.

But when Monday came, Eleanor found she could not make the visits she had wished to, nor could she send a note with one of the servants. A sudden storm had blown in during the night, bringing with it freezing temperatures and gale force winds. Though it did not snow much, the winds whipped what little fell into a blinding white frenzy, making travel impossible.

By Wednesday the storm had ceased, but it left the town bitterly cold. Eleanor, anxious to fulfill her mission, was forced to reconsider due to one of her headaches, which robbed her of her faculties for the remainder of the day. She was weak and exhausted the next morning, but at last managed to send word to the Whitmans and Miss Anderson on Thursday, inquiring after their health. The footman she dispatched on her errand returned shortly before dinner.

"Miss Anderson was too ill to receive me, ma'am, but Mrs. Whitman thanked you kindly for your concern. She said a few of the children were unwell but she hoped they would be on the mend soon."

"Did she say what was ailing them?"

"No, ma'am. But she thanked you for the basket. She said Mrs. Lewis had called on them yesterday with a parcel as well."

Eleanor smiled upon hearing this. Even when she herself was unwell, Mrs. Lewis was always thinking of others.

"Thank you, Martin."

With her footman gone, Eleanor returned to her sewing. Her nimble fingers worked deftly on the pair of trousers for her nephew, but after twenty minutes, she paused, rubbing her hands together. The room had grown cold. The house, old and drafty as it was, did not retain heat very well, and she went to add another log to the grate. She poked at the fire until the flames grew and the warmth increased. Instead of returning to her sewing, however, she went downstairs in search of her husband.

Cartwright Manor was an old stone edifice with more windows than rooms and more rooms than occupants. Though it was very grand, the interior was often gloomy and dark, especially on overcast days. Eleanor had taken great pains to bring as much light and warmth to the house as possible, making over each room on the main floor before moving upstairs to the bedrooms and salons.

She found Albert reading in a corner of the library. A cheerful fire burned in the grate as Eleanor entered the room.

"Ah!" Albert said, looking up from his book. " *'She walks in beauty, like the night of cloudless climes and starry skies; And all that's best of dark and bright meet in her aspect and her eyes,'* " he quoted softly. Eleanor laughed.

"Reading Lord Byron again?" she teased.

"No, in fact," he said, closing the book. "I was studying the philosophy of René Descartes."

"And do you find it to align with your own?"

"Not in the least," he said, rising from his chair with the assistance of his cane. "But it certainly makes for some interesting reading. What have you been doing with yourself this morning?"

"Sewing. A pair of trousers for Michael."

Albert smiled knowingly, but Eleanor continued before he could say anything. "I stopped because the room grew cold. I put another log on the fire, but we seem to be going through wood much faster than we usually do."

"Yes, I have noticed that as well. That storm seems to have sunk us into a cold spell—much colder than is usual for this time of year."

Eleanor saw him wince as he stumped his way towards her. "How is your leg?" she asked.

"Stiffer than usual. But I shall manage."

He smiled at her and offered his arm, which she took with both of her hands. Albert's leg had been crippled in a horrific accident in his youth, the same accident which had also marred his face. Though the lapse of more than thirty years since then had healed the wounds to his spirit, the physical scars remained.

They made their way to the sofa, and Eleanor sat down while

Albert added another log to the fire.

"I sent Martin with a basket for the Whitmans, and Miss Anderson," Eleanor said.

"Are they unwell?"

"They were not at church, and I was worried about them."

"I see." He sat down beside her and looked up expectantly. "And?"

"Martin said Miss Anderson was too ill to receive him, and that a few of the Whitman children were ill. But it sounds as though Mrs. Whitman was not overly concerned."

"That is encouraging, then."

"Except about Miss Anderson," Eleanor said, worrying her hands in her lap. "I should like to go and see her."

Albert rested his hand on top of hers. "You cannot risk your own health in such weather as this. Perhaps in a week or two." He paused. "How is your head?"

She sighed, looking away. "Better."

"I am glad to hear it."

The weather warmed a bit the latter part of the week, and when Sunday came again, Eleanor was anxious to see if Miss Anderson would be in attendance. But like the week before, she was not in the congregation. Nor were the Whitmans. Eleanor looked around the chapel and was alarmed to see that several other families were missing as well. Mrs. Lewis, though seated in her usual pew, was very pale, and coughed more than the previous week. Eleanor looked to Albert, who shook his head.

When the meeting ended, the Cartwrights intercepted Mrs. Lewis on her way out the door.

"Why are you not in bed?" Eleanor asked. Then, more sternly, "Even those accustomed to caring for others must be cared for at times," she said. Mrs. Lewis smiled weakly.

"It is not very Christian of you to cast my words back on me," she said. "But you are right—I should not have come. Mr. Lewis advised me to stay home, but I was stubborn and did not want to miss his sermon." She sighed, and Albert frowned.

"He will not thank you for coming, if it means that you put your health at risk," he said. "Come, let us get you home."

"He is coming," Mrs. Lewis said, and Eleanor turned to see Father Lewis across the room, struggling to get through the parishioners to his wife's side. The concern on his face was clearly evident, even from the distance.

"Good," Eleanor said, giving her friend's hand a squeeze. "Get yourself back in bed, and do not arise until you are fully recovered," she said.

"Yes, dear," Mrs. Lewis said, just as her husband arrived at her side.

They parted ways, and Eleanor took Albert's arm as they made their way to the carriage.

"The Whitmans were not in church again," she murmured.

"Nor the Kirks. Quite a few of our friends are ill, it seems."

Eleanor was silent but her mind was not at rest. When they were seated inside the carriage, she finally formed the question foremost in her mind.

"Albert," she said softly, "do you think…"

"No." His reply came swiftly, but gently. "The likelihood of another scarlet fever outbreak is not great." She relaxed, and he continued. "The weather was so mild, and then we had such a sudden chill—my guess is that the culprit is merely a product of the change in temperature. A head cold, perhaps, or a chest cold, such as Mrs. Lewis has. If it will make you easy," he said, taking her hand, "I shall inquire of Mrs. Jones, whether or not she knows anything of it."

"Oh, yes, please. Henrietta will likely know what is to be done."

But the old midwife did not have good news for the Cartwrights. Albert came in to Eleanor's room the next morning with a grim face.

"Miss Anderson has died," he said.

"Oh, no!" Eleanor's hand flew to her mouth.

Albert sighed, lowering himself into a chair. "And I have heard from Henrietta Jones. As I suspected, it is not scarlet fever."

"But?"

He heard the anxiety in her voice, and his face was grave as he replied. "Miss Anderson died of pneumonia. The Kirks have it, too. As do the Whitmans."

"Pneumonia?" she said weakly.

Albert nodded. "From influenza."

Chapter 4

The sickness spread quickly, far more quickly than anyone anticipated. Albert flatly refused to let Eleanor drive into town, fearful that she might catch the disease as well. She paced the house from morning till night, wringing her hands and fretting over her friends and loved ones until she was sick with anxiety. Albert watched her patiently, speaking softly to her when she worried herself into a frenzy. When she could stand the isolation no longer, Eleanor took herself across the way to her brother's house at Edgewood Park, after having first been assured that no one there was ill.

"Oh Eleanor, it is simply dreadful!" Beatrice greeted her.

Eleanor sat on the sofa in her sister-in-law's parlor and folded her hands in her lap. Beatrice took her place in the chair opposite, her face a picture of despair.

"You simply cannot imagine my shock, and terror, upon

hearing of the influenza. I dare not risk my precious darlings by venturing out into the neighborhood, but what is to be done? Nathaniel says I am overreacting, and that it will all clear up in a week or two, but I do not believe him."

"Nathan has always been an optimist," Eleanor agreed.

"Precisely. He does not even have the decency to worry over his own children!"

Eleanor flinched.

"I simply do not understand him," Beatrice continued. "But *you* understand, Eleanor. You know firsthand how dangerous it is to attend to those who are ill."

"Yes," Eleanor said, absently rubbing her temple.

"I must leave it to Mrs. Lewis and Mrs. Jones. They are quite capable of handling things in town, I believe. And we are so far out of the way as it is. As are you."

"Indeed."

Eleanor could think of nothing more to say, and after a few minutes Beatrice asked if Eleanor would mind if she had the children brought in. Eleanor brightened considerably.

"Of course not! I would love to see them."

Beatrice rang the bell, and presently a maid in a starched uniform came in. "Please tell Nurse MacDowell to bring the children down," she said.

A thrill coursed through Eleanor as she waited for her niece and nephew to arrive. Children had always brought her joy, but her brother's children were even more dear to her than the many others she had known. Though parting from them sharpened the pain of her own loneliness, she was never happier than when she was in their company.

Soon the parlor door opened, and the nursemaid came in carrying Cecelia on her hip. Michael bounded ahead of her into the room and dashed into his mother's arms.

"Michael! I have asked you before not to run at me," Beatrice chided, though she hugged him to her. Eleanor smiled, waiting for her turn.

"Now, go and give Auntie Nora a hug," Beatrice said, nudging him forward.

Obediently, Michael gave Eleanor a quick hug, then climbed onto the chair beside his aunt.

"I'm going to be a soldier when I grow up," he announced.

"Are you?" Eleanor replied.

"Yes. I'm going to wear a red coat and ride a horse and carry a gun with me, like Papa's."

"That sounds very exciting."

"You will do no such thing, Michael," his mother said. "You know very well that you will be a gentleman and take over the estate, like your father."

The little boy scowled. "That's boring. I want to be a soldier." He slid off the chair and plopped onto the floor, pantomiming a battle scene between his two fists. Beatrice sighed.

Cecelia was sitting on her mother's lap, but her large brown eyes were trained on Eleanor. "Tee Nowa," she lisped.

"Oh!" Eleanor cried. "Yes, my darling, Auntie Nora!" Her heart filled to bursting, and she held her arms out. Cece reached for her, too, but Beatrice snuggled her closer.

"Well done, Cece!" she cooed. "You have learned a new word! Now can you say 'Mama'? Say 'Mama,' Cece," she prodded.

"Tee Nowa," Cecelia repeated. Eleanor laughed in delight,

reaching for her again. Beatrice reluctantly gave her up.

"Cece says lots of words," Michael piped up. "But I say more words."

"That is because you are a great, big boy who has learned many things," Eleanor said solemnly. Michael nodded.

"You certainly are Mama's great, big boy," Beatrice said in a singsong voice, reaching down and wrapping her arms around him. He wriggled out of her embrace and crawled away, looking for something to do. His mother sighed again.

"I do love them, but they certainly keep me busy," Beatrice said. "Michael gets into all sorts of mischief, and it is all Nurse MacDowell and I can do to track him down and clean him up before he has escaped the nursery again."

"Little boys seem to come that way, I think," Eleanor said, kissing Cecelia's chubby fingers. "I remember Nathan always sneaking off to the kitchen or the stables when he was a boy."

"Well, that may be so," Beatrice said, rising from her place to retrieve her daughter. Cecelia fussed when she was picked up. "But Mama's little Cece is a perfect angel, aren't you, my darling?"

Cecelia began to cry, and Beatrice smiled apologetically at Eleanor. "Forgive me, Eleanor, but I believe I must attend to the children now."

"Of course," Eleanor said, rising from her place. She gave Cecelia's little arm a squeeze and called a cheery farewell to Michael, who was stalking imaginary tigers behind the drapes.

"Thank you for coming," Beatrice said.

Eleanor smiled and nodded, the familiar tightness filling her chest as she left the room.

Mrs. Lewis invited Eleanor to join her for tea a few days later, and Eleanor gladly accepted. She was most anxious to see her friend, and almost ran ahead of the maid in her haste to ensure that Mrs. Lewis was all right.

"Are you quite well?" she demanded, as soon as she entered the room. "And Father Lewis?"

"Yes, yes, my dear, we are well. My cough is all but gone, thank heavens," Mrs. Lewis said, embracing the younger woman. Eleanor breathed a sigh of relief. "I only wish I could say the same for the rest of the parish."

"How bad is it?"

"Very bad. The Kirks have it, and so do the Bryants. The Whitmans, of course—I worry for them—and the Fairchilds."

Eleanor pressed her lips together.

"Henrietta is nearly beside herself. So many are ill, and there is only so much she can do. She is coming for tea as well. I thought it would be a good chance for us to discuss the needs of the parish, all together."

They did not wait long. Mrs. Jones was soon there, pulling off a heavy woolen muffler and extricating herself from her many layers.

"Gracious, have you ever seen the likes?" the old midwife said as they sat down. "It's been nigh on twenty years since an influenza epidemic like this spread through town. London, of course, is afflicted far more often. Norwich, even. But here, in our community?" She shook her head. "I'm bone-weary, friends. Bone-weary. I'm far too old to be called at all hours of the day and night to see after the sick. I have a hard enough time with the occasional birthing, you know."

"Which is exactly what I wanted to discuss," Mrs. Lewis broke in. "Now that I am well myself, I am ready to help where I can. Who is in the greatest need?"

Mrs. Jones snorted. "Who is not, might be the better question. Nearly all the families in town have been afflicted in some way. Only a matter of time before it spreads to the outlying farms."

"What can be done to prevent its spreading?" Eleanor asked. Mrs. Jones shrugged.

"Not much, I reckon. Time of year, you know. And the weather."

"The weather certainly makes it difficult," Mrs. Lewis said. "But as it is not in our control, let us consider the matters that are. Who is the most ill, and what can we do for them?"

"Well, Miss Anderson, God rest her, developed pneumonia pretty quick. Little Matthew Whitman has it now, too. That's where the danger comes in. That's what we're fighting against."

"To prevent pneumonia?" Eleanor asked.

"Aye."

"And how do we do so?" Mrs. Lewis asked.

"We have to keep it from settling in the lungs," Mrs. Jones replied. "Keep them warm. Keep them coughing. Nurse them back to health before it has a chance to take hold."

Mrs. Lewis nodded. "We shall do our best. Where should we focus our efforts?"

"The Whitmans, Kirks, Bryants, and Fairchilds all have several family members in various states of illness. The Manwills, too."

28

The Manwill family was relatively new to Littleton. They settled in the neighborhood a few years back, but Mr. Manwill ran off and abandoned his family about a year ago. Mrs. Manwill, a tiny, delicate thing, took in washing and ironing in an attempt to put food on the table for her two little boys, but they mostly lived on the charity of the parish. Her youngest son was only a few months older than Cecelia.

Mrs. Lewis was nodding. "I have visited the Kirks, and the Bryants."

"I sent a basket to the Whitmans," Eleanor said. "And I will check on the Manwills."

"Good. I received a note from Mrs. Grantham just before I came, and it sounds likely they might be ill as well. I'll be heading over there after tea," Mrs. Jones said, shaking her head.

Eleanor groaned, while Mrs. Lewis poured a fresh cup of tea for Mrs. Jones. "Is there anything more we can do?" she asked.

The midwife-turned-emergency-physician shook her head, her face grave. "Just pray the winter doesn't last long. I've a feeling we haven't seen the worst of it yet."

Eleanor, Mrs. Lewis, and Mrs. Jones decided to split the neighborhood into thirds: the minister and his wife would see to the families north and west of town, Mrs. Jones would care for those in Littleton proper and to the east, and Eleanor would care for their friends and neighbors to the south. They parted ways in high spirits, eager to help and optimistic for the outcome. Eleanor, happy to have found a purpose once more, met with opposition as soon as she arrived home.

"No," Albert said, before she had even finished explaining things to him.

"But Albert, the town needs me!"

"You are not well. You cannot risk your health, Eleanor."

"I am quite well enough to offer comfort and compassion," she retorted. "And if I tire more easily than I once did, who is to say it is not the effect of getting on in years?"

Albert allowed himself a small smile. "You are *not* getting on in years, Eleanor."

His softened look gave her courage. "Please, Albert. I need to do this."

He groaned and stumped to the window, his cane thumping on the floor with familiar resonance. "Why must you?" he said, looking out the window instead of at her.

She walked slowly to his side and looked up at him. His profile, from the right, was perfect and unmarred. There was no evidence of the accident which took his mother's life, or the scars he bore on the opposite side of his face. Eleanor gazed at him until he turned and looked at her.

"Because I need to feel whole," she said softly. "You often speak of feeling whole only after love came into your life."

"After *you* came into my life."

She smiled. "After I brought love into your life," she amended. Her look grew serious, and her voice more earnest. "For many years now, I have felt broken. Without children of our own, I have felt as if life had no meaning, and I no purpose in it."

She paused, and he covered the hand which she had laid on his arm with his. "I believe this endeavor can help to heal the ache in my heart," she said quietly. "I know that it cannot repair it completely, but seeing to the needs of others, and helping those who cannot help themselves is a step towards wholeness. And I need that, Albert."

For a long time he looked at her, his gaze full of both admiration and fear. Finally he sighed. "What if you become ill?" he asked.

Eleanor drew a breath. "Then I shall cease my ministry and come home at once. And that shall be the end of it."

"At the first sign of illness?"

"Yes. You have my word."

He sighed again. "Very well. I can see how this might help. But I am counting on you to take great care, my dear. I cannot lose you."

Eleanor stretched up onto her toes and brushed a kiss on his cheek. "I shall. I promise."

Chapter 5

The weather must have known what the women had planned, for the next few days were bitterly cold. A northern wind blew down from the sea, chilling every corner of the town. The drafty halls and soaring ceilings of Cartwright Manor were no match for the freezing temperatures, and Eleanor and Albert holed themselves up in the library, where a roaring fire and hundreds of books kept them relatively comfortable throughout the day.

The cold snap did not last long, however, and soon Eleanor and Albert were carting loads of wood and coal to various families in the neighborhood. Mrs. Whitman cried when they arrived, declaring that her husband had been stricken ill, and they were running dangerously low on firewood.

"Bless you!" she cried between her tears.

"There now, Mrs. Whitman. It is all right," Eleanor said, comforting her. "We have plenty of firewood, and I have brought some soup besides. I shall set it on the stove to keep warm until you need it."

"Thank you, Mrs. Cartwright. And Mr. Cartwright. You are angels, the both of you."

"How is your son, Mrs. Whitman?" Albert asked.

"Matthew is no better. But Joseph is on the mend, I believe."

The Cartwrights did not stay long, but promised to call again soon. After another brief stop to check on the Harrisons, they finally pulled up to the small house where the Manwills lived.

It was on the outskirts of town, down a short lane and through a little copse of trees which hid it from view. A beautiful maple tree grew alongside the house, its strong branches reaching up and over the dilapidated roof. Eleanor knew it provided much-needed shade in the summer, but at the moment, its naked boughs were spindly and harsh, cutting the sky into broken shards of milky blue.

Eleanor heard coughing coming from inside the house as soon as they stepped down from the carriage. She looked to Albert, whose jaw tightened. Their knock was answered by the timid Mrs. Manwill, who only opened the door a crack.

"Mrs. Manwill?" Eleanor said. "We heard your family was ill, and we wanted to see how you were doing."

Mrs. Manwill shook her head, but before she could respond she was overcome by a coughing fit. Albert visibly stiffened, and Eleanor fought the urge to step back. When she regained some control, Mrs. Manwill rasped out, "No, no—we are too ill. You should not risk your health."

She began to shut the door, but Eleanor put her hand out. "Please, Mrs. Manwill, you should be in bed. Let me help."

"Eleanor…" Albert said.

"Let *us* help," she said with feeling, her eyes pleading as they sought Albert's. He sighed.

"We have firewood, Mrs. Manwill," he said.

"And soup," Eleanor added.

The young mother looked up at them from hollow eyes, but at last she stepped back and opened the door. She began coughing again, and Eleanor gently guided her to the small sofa in the front room and helped her lie down. More coughing could be heard coming through a doorway off to the left, and Eleanor looked to Albert.

"Would you see about the children, please?" she asked.

He nodded and went to investigate, while Eleanor bustled about the kitchen, setting the soup on the stove and boiling water for tea. She brought a bowl of warm broth and slowly spooned it into Mrs. Manwill's mouth.

"How long have you been sick?" she asked.

Mrs. Manwill swallowed. "A week. I think."

"And the children?"

"The baby's been sick longer than me. Henry just came down a few days ago."

Eleanor finished feeding her the soup and tucked a blanket around her. She was just going to find Albert when he emerged from the back room looking grave.

"How are they?" Eleanor asked, her voice low.

"The older boy was coughing. I gave him some water and made him as comfortable as I could. The baby, however…" He shook his head.

She drew in a sharp breath. "Is it… was he…" Eleanor could

not bear to form the words.

"He was still alive. But I do not think for long." He glanced over Eleanor's shoulder at Mrs. Manwill, who had drifted off to sleep.

Bracing herself, Eleanor crossed the room and pushed upon the bedroom door. A dirty blanket hung across the window, and it took a moment for her eyes to adjust in the dim light. She looked around. The room was sparsely furnished, with only one small bed, an old bureau, and a makeshift cradle occupying the space. Burrowed underneath the blankets on the bed was six-year-old Henry, whose bright blue eyes were watching her.

"Are... are you an angel?" he whispered as she crouched beside him.

His question caught Eleanor by surprise. "No, I am Mrs. Cartwright."

"Oh."

She could not tell if he was disappointed with her answer. She brushed a lock of dark hair away from his face.

"Were you expecting an angel?" she asked softly.

"No. But Mother says the angels watch over us, and you're just about the prettiest lady I've ever seen. So I thought you must be an angel."

"I believe that is the nicest thing anyone has ever said to me," Eleanor said, swallowing past the lump in her throat.

He grinned, and she caught a flash of straight white teeth before he bent his head, overcome by a cough. She stood and reached for a tin of water on the bureau, waiting until his cough subsided. She help him sit up and gave him the cup, noting how thin he was. As he drank, she heard soft wheezing coming from the cradle. She stood and went to the small crib on the other side of the room. Looking inside, her eyes filled with tears.

The baby was sleeping, his long, thick lashes brushing the tops of his ashen cheeks. His perfect little lips were blue, but his chest rose and fell in the tiniest movement, proof that he still clung to the delicate thread of life. Gently, Eleanor reached in and picked him up. His body was limp.

Tucking the blankets around him, she cradled him to her chest, humming softly as she swayed from side to side. His breathing was shallow and labored. Her throat was tight, and she could not help but bend down and softly kiss his clammy forehead. Turning around, she saw Henry in bed, watching her.

"You *are* an angel," he said, his voice awed. "Mother said an angel would come take James to Heaven when he died."

His innocent voice was so sure, so confident, that it tore at Eleanor's heart. With a strangled sob, she bowed her head and wept.

Chapter 6

Albert paced the length of the breakfast room, worry making him move too quickly and haste making him stumble. He forced himself to stop when he knocked into the end of the table for the third time, sending shooting pains through his lame leg. Cursing under his breath, he sat down heavily in a chair, his mind still racing.

Eleanor.

When Eleanor first proposed the idea of caring for the sick, the risk to her physical health had been foremost on his mind. But after their visit to the Manwills yesterday, he was more concerned about the risk to her heart. It was delicate, he knew, but seeing her ashen face and hearing her sobs had nearly undone him. He could not bear to see her suffer even more than she already had.

Albert stood abruptly as Eleanor entered the room. Her eyes were swollen and red, and she moved gingerly. He frowned.

"Nora, you should be in bed," he said. But his wife only shook her head, then winced as the movement sent daggers into her temples. He raised one eyebrow at her.

"You were crying all night," he said softly, moving to stand beside her. "You need your rest."

"I must speak with Mrs. Jones," Eleanor replied, lifting a hand to her forehead. "She needs to know about the Manwills."

"Can it not wait until tomorrow?"

There was a long pause before Eleanor spoke again. "Tomorrow might be too late," she said softly.

Albert nodded. "Would you care for some breakfast?"

"Some tea and toast is all, please. I want to be on my way."

Albert poured her a cup and added honey and cream, knowing that is how she always took it.

"Since you are insistent upon leaving the house when you are obviously feeling unwell," Albert raised his brow, daring her to contradict him, "I must beg to be allowed to accompany you."

Eleanor smiled through her pain. "You need not beg. You know I am always glad of your company, Albert."

He smiled grimly, the movement pulling his lips down on one side and up on the other. "And if I chose to remain here? Would the pleasure of my company be enough to persuade you to stay home with me?"

Her eyes grew bright. "Unfortunately, no."

"I thought not."

A quarter hour later they were on their way. Mrs. Jones was just leaving through the front gate of her house when their carriage pulled up.

"Mrs. Jones, where are you off to?" Eleanor called, opening

the door of the coach.

"The Granthams."

"Climb in," Albert said. "We shall give you a ride."

The old woman climbed inside the carriage and sat down beside Eleanor. "My thanks," she said, settling into her seat. "My old bones don't like the walk in this cold."

"Mrs. Jones," Eleanor said as the carriage started forward. "We visited the Manwills yesterday."

"And how are they faring?"

"Poorly," Albert broke in. "Mrs. Manwill is quite ill, and the baby at death's door."

Eleanor bit her lip, and the midwife clucked her tongue. "I was afraid of that," she said. "Poor mite never stood a chance, small and malnourished as he was."

"Can nothing be done?" Eleanor asked.

"No. Not if he's as bad as you say." She turned to Albert. "How was his color?"

"Gray. His lips were blue, and he was barely breathing."

Mrs. Jones shook her head. "God rest him," she murmured.

The trio was silent until the carriage stopped in front of Grantham's Mercantile. Albert stepped out and offered Mrs. Jones his hand. She thanked him and turned back to face Eleanor.

" 'Tis sad when the little ones die," she said, "but that is the way of it sometimes."

"Can we not send for the doctor in Norwich?" Eleanor asked.

Mrs. Jones snorted. "To hurry him on his way? Not while I have breath. More often than not, doctor's 'cures' kill their patients faster than the disease would have. We're better off to treat the illness as best we can ourselves." She waved and strode off.

Though she was weary in body and spirit, Eleanor insisted that they make a few visits on the way back to the house. The Sotherbys were well, and the Kirks were faring better, which was happy news to hear after such a melancholy morning. The Cartwrights returned to their home relatively cheerful, and Eleanor accepted Albert's request to rest before dinner.

When she came downstairs a few hours later, she heard voices in the drawing room. Turning her steps thither, she was pleasantly surprised to find her brother's family gathered therein.

"Nora! Come to join the fun at last, eh?" her brother teased, standing as she entered.

"Had I known you were coming to call, I would have come down sooner," she replied, making her way towards Beatrice and Cecelia. Her niece's chubby little arms reached up for her, and Eleanor picked her up, nuzzling her cheek.

"Auntie Nora, guess what?" Michael cried, hopping down from his place on the sofa next to his mother. "I have a loose tooth!"

"Do you really?" Eleanor cried in mock amazement. She bent her head to inspect the anomaly, and nodded gravely as he demonstrated how precariously it was attached.

"Michael! Where are your manners?" his mother chided. But the boy merely grinned and scampered off towards his father.

"Tee Nowa," Cecelia lisped, clutching the shoulder of Eleanor's dress. Eleanor cooed at her niece, feeling the ache in her heart subside as she held her.

"Albert tells us you have joined Mrs. Lewis and Mrs. Jones in an effort to cure the sick," Nathaniel said.

"Do you think that wise, considering your health?" Beatrice asked.

Eleanor smiled. "I thank you for your concern, but I assure you that I am quite well."

"And she has promised to call off the rescue and return home at the first sign that she is falling ill herself," Albert added, raising his eyebrows at his wife.

"Albert is helping as well," Eleanor said. "He sent Martin over to the Whitmans to chop wood the other day. And we have been delivering coal to those in need."

"I could do with an occupation myself," Nathaniel said. "I am bored out of my mind, holed up at Edgewood as we are. Perhaps I should call on the Bryants and see if they need any assistance."

"Send one of the servants," his wife said, a note of anxiety in her voice. "It is risk enough attending church when so many are stricken. I have half a mind to stay home until it has all cleared up."

"Do you think we should send for the doctor in Norwich?" Nathaniel asked.

Eleanor hesitated. "I do not know. Mrs. Jones seems to think that a physician will only make the people worse."

Nathaniel shrugged. "If it is as bad as you say, perhaps he could help."

"Perhaps."

Eleanor did not want to talk of doctors and sickness anymore. Her tender spirit was still smarting from her experience at the Manwills, and at present, all she wanted to do was cuddle her niece and listen to her nephew prattle on about the royal army.

She exchanged pleasantries with her sister-in-law, while the gentleman talked of politics and the weather.

"Will you be joining us for dinner?" Eleanor asked Beatrice. "You know you are always welcome."

Beatrice smiled. "Thank you, we should be delighted."

Michael hurried to his aunt's side. "Can we have ginger biscuits, please?" he asked, his voice hopeful.

"Not for dinner," Eleanor replied, and his face fell. "But I think we can go and have some now if you would like."

Michael crowed in delight, which earned him a gentle reprimand from his mother, but Eleanor merely laughed. Shifting Cecelia to one hip, she took his hand.

"Here, let me take Cece," Beatrice said.

The women took the children off to the kitchen, leaving the men behind. Albert watched them go, a sad expression on his marred face.

"She loves those children," he murmured, almost to himself. Nathaniel nodded.

"And they simply adore their aunt. Beatrice is quite jealous."

"Jealous? Of Eleanor?" Albert said, incredulous. Nathaniel shrugged.

"You know how Eleanor is—she has such a way with children. Mothering comes so naturally to her, and Beatrice wishes she were the same."

"Eleanor would give anything to have children of her own," Albert said.

"You may have children yet."

Albert shook his head. "Perhaps. But I am beginning to think the good Lord has something else in mind for us."

Chapter 7

Their guests left just as it was getting dark and a fierce wind began to blow. Freezing rain pelted the windows, running in heavy rivulets down the glass before pooling on the sill. After supper, Albert and Eleanor retired to the library, to spend a cozy evening in front of the fire. Eleanor sat quietly knitting, while Albert read aloud from one of his books. Outside, the storm continued to rage, but inside, all was calm.

The storm had blown itself out by morning, but a steady drizzle promised to fall all the next day. Half-frozen puddles littered the road, reflecting the solid gray blanket of the sky overhead. Inside the manor it was dark as twilight, and Eleanor shivered in the gloom. The cold stone of the walls and floors incubated the house like an icebox.

Eleanor pulled her shawl more tightly around her shoulders as she descended the stairs for breakfast. Albert was waiting for her on the landing.

"Good morning, my dear. How do you feel?"

She shivered. "Like an icicle in midwinter." Albert laughed and pulled her into his arms. "Mm, this is better," she said, closing her eyes.

With Albert's strong arms around her, Eleanor felt almost whole. The fractures in her heart knit together, safe in his embrace. But all too soon he released her, and the fissures opened up again, gaping and raw. She took his arm as they went down to breakfast.

They enjoyed a hearty meal of freshly baked bread, sausages, tea, and preserves. For a short while, Eleanor almost forgot the sadness and sickness spread about the town, enjoying the time spent with her husband. They took their breakfast alone, as they always had.

As she feared they always would.

Just as the Cartwrights were finishing their meal, the butler entered the room. "Miss Henrietta Jones is awaiting you in the drawing room," he said with a bow.

"Thank you, Pritchett, tell her we shall be right in," Eleanor replied.

"Were you expecting her?" Albert asked, helping her from the table.

"No." Eleanor bit her lip. "I hope it is not bad news."

Albert frowned. "We shall find out soon enough," he said.

Though she had only been waiting a few minutes, they found their guest dozing in the armchair next to the fire, her head tipped back and her mouth slightly agape. Albert chuckled, but Eleanor shook her head.

"Poor Mrs. Jones! She must be exhausted. I hate to wake her."
Albert cleared his throat loudly, and with a start the old
woman sat up.

"Oh! Forgive me, I must have drifted off," she said, stifling a
yawn. " 'Tis nice to visit a home where there's no one ill to care
for."

"Would you like some tea, Mrs, Jones?" Eleanor asked, taking
the seat across from her.

"Thank you, no. I haven't much time, only stopped to tell you
there's been another death. The Manwill baby is gone—left for
Heaven this morning. I stopped at the parsonage to let Father
Lewis know, but I thought you'd like to know as well."

Eleanor covered her mouth, tears shining in her eyes. "The
poor, dear thing," she murmured.

Mrs. Jones gave her a sad smile. "That is the way of things,
Mrs. Cartwright," she said. "At least now he is at rest."

Eleanor nodded, the movement causing her tears to break free
and run down her cheeks. Albert went to stand beside her, and
Mrs. Jones stood to go.

"How are the Granthams?" Albert asked.

"Mr. Grantham is on the mend, but now his wife and son are
ill," Mrs. Jones sighed.

"And the Whitmans?"

"Not out of the woods yet."

"Thank you, Mrs. Jones," Eleanor said, drying her eyes.
"Please let us know if there is more we can do."

Mrs. Jones nodded and took her leave. After she had gone,
Eleanor excused herself to seek solace in her room. Albert's brow
furrowed in concern.

"Can I have anything sent up for you?" he asked.

"No, thank you. Just a bit of peace is all I need."

She brushed a kiss on his scarred cheek and climbed the stairs to her bedchamber. Her heart ached for the Manwill baby, and even more for his poor mother. What pain she must be experiencing! What agony, to lose a child! Eleanor's own heart felt the prick of emptiness, but she knew it could not compare to the pain of losing a child one has cared for and loved as a mother. She sat on the edge of her bed and wept for a long, long, time.

When her tears had ceased, Eleanor dried her face and crossed the room to a small black trunk below the window. Kneeling in front of it, she undid the brass buckles and lifted the heavy lid.

Folded carefully and arranged in neat little piles was a full baby layette. Tiny knit stockings, small lacy bonnets, and beribboned dresses were waiting, perfect and pristine, for the baby who would not come. Eleanor fingered the folds of a creamy yellow gown, tears streaming down her face. She put it gently aside, looking through the trunk until she found the article she sought. It was near the bottom, as it had been one of the first things she made as a new bride.

It was a beautiful christening gown, made of ivory silk and trimmed with intricate lace. Satin ribbons festooned the long embroidered skirt, which hung almost to the floor as she lifted it into the light. Memories and emotions flooded her mind, fighting for dominance in her heart.

Gathering the garment carefully into her arms, she rose from the floor and sat on the bed. She spread the garment out on her lap, caressing the pleats and folds she had labored so carefully to create. Her tears were slow and steady, but with a firm hand she folded the dress into a neat little bundle and carried it out of the room.

Albert looked up as she walked into the library. "I thought you were going to rest for the remainder of the morning," he said in surprise. His welcoming smile faded as he noticed her puffy eyes, and then what she held in her arms. By the time she reached his side, he was on his feet.

"Is that…?" His voice trailed off expectantly, and when Eleanor nodded, he opened his arms. She stepped into his embrace, carefully guarding the garment she held.

"I would like to give it to Mrs. Manwill," she said, her voice barely above a whisper.

His only response was to hold her tighter.

Eleanor did not trust her voice for several minutes. When she was sure it would be steady, she took a deep breath. "I thought she would like to have it. For the baby."

"You spent months on that piece," Albert said, his voice soft. When she merely nodded, he asked, "Would you make another?"

Eleanor did not reply right away. "Perhaps," she said at last, but Albert knew by the set of her jaw that she would not. In laying the Manwill baby to rest in the dress, Eleanor was laying her hopes and dreams to rest, too. He reached a hand out and fingered the silky folds.

"I always wanted to have a son," he said, his voice husky. "An heir to the estate, and the Cartwright name."

Eleanor choked on a sob.

"I remember when you made this," he continued. "So many hours. So many evenings." He paused, clearing his throat. "It is beautiful. I am sure Mrs. Manwill will appreciate it."

Eleanor merely nodded, and he handed her his handkerchief.

"Would you like me to go with you when you take it to her?" he asked gently.

"Yes, please," she murmured. "It is *our* offering, after all," she said. Then, hesitantly, "Is it not?"

Albert swallowed. "Yes," he said, his voice catching. "Yes, it is."

Chapter 8

The horses' breath hung in haphazard clouds around their heads as the carriage pulled up in front of the Manwill cottage. Barely a wisp of smoke drifted up from the chimney, and Eleanor pulled her cloak tightly about her as Albert helped her out of the vehicle. Their boots crunched on the frozen ground as they made their way to the front door and knocked.

There was no answer.

Albert and Eleanor exchanged glances, and Albert knocked again, louder. "Mrs. Manwill?" he called. "It is the Cartwrights."

Just when Eleanor was reaching for the handle, the door swung open.

"Thank goodness you've come," Father Lewis said.

He stepped back to let them in, and Albert hurried to stoke the dying fire. Eleanor looked around. "Where is Mrs. Manwill?"

Father Lewis shook his head. "She is in the bedroom, with the baby. She is not doing well, but I cannot convince her to let me take the little one. She won't give him up."

Eleanor's throat tightened, and she swallowed. "And Henry?"

"Mrs. Lewis took him home in the carriage. He is doing much better."

Breathing a sigh of relief, Eleanor pulled off her gloves and removed her cloak. When she turned to cross the room, Father Lewis held out a hand.

"Mrs. Cartwright…"

"Yes?"

The minister's grave face said what his words could not, and Eleanor nodded. Steeling herself, she crossed to the bedroom door and gently knocked. When there was no reply, she slowly pushed it open.

Mrs. Manwill was sitting up in Henry's bed, cradling her infant son in her arms. Her eyes were closed and her breathing was shallow. Eleanor noted the same grayish tint to her skin as she had observed in little James.

"Mrs. Manwill?" Eleanor said quietly, not wishing to startle her.

The woman's eyelids fluttered.

"Mrs. Manwill, I've brought something for you. For James."

She sat on the edge of the bed, and slowly the woman beside her opened her eyes. "James?" she whispered. Eleanor nodded.

"Yes, Mrs. Manwill, for James."

"James," Mrs. Manwill said again, her voice cracking. "James is…"

But she could say no more. Her face crumpled and she fell forward. Eleanor reached out just in time to stop her from toppling off the bed. Mrs. Manwill remained hunched over her son, broken sobs wracking her body as she gasped for air.

Eleanor put an arm around her shoulders, her own chest tight. "I know, Mrs. Manwill, I know. I am so sorry."

"My baby, my baby," Mrs. Manwill moaned.

Eleanor held her more tightly.

When Mrs. Manwill's sobs subsided, Eleanor helped her sit up again. Mrs. Manwill's lips were blue, and she leaned against Eleanor as if she had lost all her strength.

Carefully, Eleanor reached a slender arm down to retrieve the parcel that had fallen from her lap. She picked it up and set it beside her on the bed. Mrs. Manwill lifted her head.

"For James?" she whispered.

"Yes, Mrs. Manwill. It is something for James. Would you like to see it?"

Without waiting for a response, Eleanor untied the ribbon holding the bundle of fabric together and unfolded the gown. Holding it up in the air, she smiled sadly and looked at the woman beside her. Her eyes were glassy.

" 'Tis beautiful," Mrs. Manwill murmured.

"Thank you," Eleanor said, her voice soft. "It took me many hours to make it."

"For... James?"

Eleanor shook her head. "I had meant this for my own child someday," she said slowly. "A little angel to call my own. But it would please me very much if you would accept it as a gift, for your little angel."

The grieving mother choked on her reply. "Oh, yes. Yes, yes. Thank you, Mrs. Cartwright." She started to cry again. "Father

Lewis came to take little James away, but I couldn't let him go. I couldn't bear to think of my little boy, dirty and naked and blue. I couldn't—"

Eleanor pressed her handkerchief into Mrs. Manwill's hand. "Hush, now. It is all right. James will look beautiful. And he shan't be dirty, for Mrs. Lewis will see to it that he's bathed."

Mrs. Manwill took a shaky breath. "Yes. That will do." She looked up at Eleanor. "And I will see him in Heaven," she whispered.

Eleanor's voice caught. "Yes, Mrs. Manwill. You shall be with him in Heaven."

The dying woman's face relaxed, and she closed her eyes. "I shall be with him in Heaven," she murmured, leaning back against the wall. Drawing a shaky breath, she closed her eyes.

She did not open them again.

Chapter 9

Mrs. Manwill was laid to rest with her infant son in her arms, dressed in the christening gown Eleanor had labored over so carefully . Eleanor was too shaken by their deaths to attend the funeral, but insisted that Albert go to pay their respects.

The service was short and ill-attended, which made Albert glad he came. As far as he knew, Mrs. Manwill had no near relations, and aside from himself and the Lewises, the only other person in attendance was Henrietta Jones. The old midwife coughed through most of the service, and he went directly to her side at the conclusion of it.

"Mrs. Jones, are you unwell?" he asked, leaning upon his cane.

"No rest for the weary," she said. "But I'm afraid it's catching up to me." She turned away, coughing into her handkerchief.

"Dear Mrs. Jones, please go home and rest," Mrs. Lewis said, coming up to stand beside them. "What will we do if *you* are stricken ill?"

"Same as we're doing for the others: rest and warmth and keep me coughing, and if that don't work, put me in a pine box and bury me before sundown."

"Mrs. Jones!"

The midwife chuckled at the appalled look on Mrs. Lewis's face. "Forgive me, Constance, but a little humor can go a long way to cure someone, you know." She did not wait for the murmured rebuke she knew was forthcoming, but instead waved a hand and started walking away. "Send me word if you've a mind to. I'm heading home to rest my bones for a time." She coughed all the way to the church door.

Mrs. Lewis sighed and shook her head. "What shall we do with her, Mr. Cartwright?"

Albert chuckled. "Well, she did say to put her in—"

"Don't you dare repeat it!" Mrs. Lewis cried, laughing tightly.

"Repeat what?" Father Lewis asked, walking up.

"Oh, nothing of consequence," Mrs. Lewis said, shooting a look at Albert. He smoothed his face into a suitably somber expression, and was rewarded when her lips twitched.

"Mr. Cartwright," Mrs. Lewis said, deftly turning the conversation, "there is a delicate matter we would like to discuss with you."

"Oh?"

"Indeed," the minister said, taking up the conversation. "We had hoped to discuss it with both you and your wife, but since Mrs. Cartwright is not here, you shall have to account for her opinion as well as yours."

Albert bowed. "I shall do my best."

"As you know, Mrs. Manwill is survived by her oldest child, Henry, whose father has not been seen in over a year. We plan to send out inquiries, but we know not the best way to go about doing so."

"Allow me. My solicitor in Norwich has connections that may prove useful in the search for Henry's father."

"Thank you, Mr. Cartwright, that is most encouraging."

In the silence that followed, the minister and his wife exchanged hesitant glances, and Albert's eyes narrowed.

"There is more?"

"Yes," Father Lewis said, clearing his throat. "You see, with Mr. Manwill unavailable at present…"

"And Mrs. Manwill laid to rest—"

"—and no other family in as suitable a position—"

"—indeed, with all the sickness spread about—"

"You want us to take the boy."

Albert said it with no emotion, though his eyes were wary.

Mrs. Lewis grasped his arm. "Only temporarily."

"Until we can locate his father, you see," the minister added.

Albert's gaze flickered between the two of them. Mrs. Lewis wore a hopeful expression on her plain face, but her husband's somber gaze made him pause.

Could they take Henry into their home? *Should* they take him?

Albert knew how sharply his mother's death could form the boy, especially after being abandoned by his father. Albert had been seven at the time his own mother died, but Henry was only four. Would it be easier for the younger child? More difficult? In his short life, Henry's family situation had already been quite challenging, and if he went to another poor home, his life may continue on a downward path. But if the Cartwrights took him in…

He let out a sigh, rubbing a hand over his eyes. "All right. Let us say that we take him in…"

Mrs. Lewis clapped her hands together in delight, a smile wreathing her face. Her husband smiled in relief.

"…until his father can be located. What then?" Albert looked sharply at the minister, whose smile faded.

"You may request guardianship, of course. His father may be willing to grant it."

Albert raised his brow. "And if he does not?" He looked from one anxious face to the other. "If his father wishes, he can take him away, and there will be nothing we can do to stop him."

When the Lewises made no answer, he dropped his voice, his look serious.

"I will make no promises," he said. "I will let Eleanor decide the boy's fate."

Mrs. Lewis released a breath, smiling once more. "Eleanor will take him in. I am sure of it."

"You have more confidence than I do, Mrs. Lewis," Albert said, his face impassive.

"You doubt the kindness and generosity of your wife's heart?" Father Lewis asked, surprise coloring his tone.

"I do not doubt the *kindness* of her heart, but I do doubt her heart's ability to heal if it is broken again," Albert said with feeling. "It has been torture enough to remain childless these many years, when all she longs for are children of her own. How do you think she would feel, if she were to take in a child and raise him as her own, only to have him ripped from her arms by another's whim?"

Silence was his answer, and Albert shook his head.

"I will not subject her to such pain by any decision of mine," he said gently. "Eleanor must decide."

Eleanor was waiting in the library when Albert returned home. He paused upon seeing her there as he opened the door.

"I thought you would still be in your room," he said.

Eleanor smiled weakly. "It was too dark and cold. I needed some comfort and warmth while I waited for you."

"And did you find it?"

She looked down at the book in her lap. "Not really. *Jane Eyre* is more melancholy than I remember it being."

Albert chuckled, making his way across the room. The smile on his scarred face faded, but Eleanor was not alarmed. She was too accustomed to it now to be frightened of the permanent scowl on one side of his face.

She arose, greeting her husband with a kiss. "How was the service?"

"Everything that was proper. Mrs. Manwill and James were laid to rest together."

"Oh, good. I was hoping that would be the case."

Eleanor sat down, folding and unfolding her hands in her lap. Albert watched her, wondering how she would react to the request he knew he must put before her.

Sitting in the chair next to hers, Albert reached out and took one of her hands in both of his own. She looked up, a sad smile on her lips, and Albert cleared his throat.

"Father Lewis and his wife spoke with me after the funeral," he said.

"Oh?"

"Yes. They requested my help in locating Mr. Manwill, to inform him of the deaths of his wife and infant son, and his responsibility to his older son, Henry."

"Oh."

Eleanor's face paled, and Albert squeezed her hand. "Until he can be located, however, there is concern over who is to care for the child."

"The Lewises, of course," Eleanor said, almost before Albert had finished speaking.

"The Lewises are getting older, and no one would be home to properly care for him. You know how busy they are with the parish."

"The Medfords—"

"—have seven mouths to feed already," Albert said gently.

Eleanor swallowed.

"The Whitmans are still ill," she whispered.

"As are the Smiths."

Abruptly she stood and paced away from him, retreating to the window to gaze out upon the frozen landscape. She hugged herself, slowly rubbing her hand up and down her arm.

"Eleanor," Albert said, his voice soft. "I would not give the Lewises an answer. I told them that you must decide."

She looked over her shoulder at him. "If it were up to you, and you alone, would you take him in?"

He answered with his silence, and she turned away again.

The quiet stretched between them, tense and cold, like the thin shell of ice over a pond. Albert went to stand behind her, putting his hands on her shoulders.

"You have a way with children, Eleanor," he said gently. "It is a gift I have rarely seen in anyone else."

She stared out the window as if she had not heard.

"And you have the heart of a mother, which is what Henry needs."

She placed a hand over her mouth, stifling a sob.

"Perhaps..." He hesitated. "Perhaps God has answered our prayers in another way."

Her startled eyes looked up at him.

"He would not be our son," she said. "His father could come at any time to claim him."

"Yes. But if we could ease his suffering, however temporarily; if we could provide him with a place to call home, and treat him as our son, not our guest..."

His voice trailed off, and she looked away. For a long time nothing else was said, and Albert wondered if he had pushed too hard. He did not want to cause her pain, and yet, he felt in his heart that this was right. Henry needed them.

And Eleanor needed Henry.

Albert knew that Eleanor enjoyed a bit of vicarious motherhood through her interactions with her brother's children, but it was not the same thing. She was not with them, day in and day out, to calm their fears and congratulate them in their triumphs. She did not tuck them in at night, nor kiss their sleeping faces, nor answer their cries in the morning. She was not their mother, however badly she may wish to be.

But Henry needed a mother, and she could be his.

If Eleanor was willing to open her heart, Albert knew that this arrangement could be the very thing to heal the pain of childlessness. It could help. But it could also go terribly wrong.

What if Henry would not love her? He dismissed the thought almost the moment it formed. Everyone loved Eleanor. Especially children. But what if Eleanor could not love Henry? Or worse— what if she did, and then his father came to take him away?

Albert closed his eyes, silently cursing himself for bringing it up. He should have told the Lewises no. Offered to find another family to take him in. Anything but subject Eleanor to further heartbreak.

He dropped his hands to his side and turned away, retrieving his cane which he'd left leaning against his chair. When he was almost to the door, her voice called him back.

"He may come," she said, still looking out the window. "He may come until his father can be located. But then he must go. He will not be our son, for he already has a father. He cannot stay with us."

Chapter 10

A note was dispatched to the parsonage, informing the Lewises that Albert and Eleanor would arrive the next morning to take Henry home with them. When the appointed time arrived, Eleanor insisted that they visit some of the sick families along the way before collecting their ward.

They found the Bryants both in bed, the illness having settled in their lungs. Eleanor placed cold compresses on their foreheads, listening to their labored breathing with a furrowed brow. Albert stoked the fire, and promised to stop by later in the afternoon with a load of firewood so they would remain warm.

The Murdoch family was faring better. With six children ranging in age from four to fourteen, some one or other of them had been ill since the influenza epidemic first hit the town. Two of the children and Mr. Murdoch were stricken at the moment, but Eleanor found them in capable hands. A fire roared in the hearth, warming the small but comfortable home, and Mrs. Murdoch assured the Cartwrights they had plenty of food.

"If this dreadful cold would only cease!" she lamented, ladling soup into bowls and setting them on the table for her other children. "There's not been a chill this long in my memory."

"Nor mine," Eleanor said.

"Let us hope we are near the end of it," Albert said. "If the weather warms up, perhaps the sick will finally get well."

Albert and Eleanor were on their way again, after Mrs. Murdoch assured them she would send at once to Cartwright Manor if they had a need. Eleanor's stomach turned and twisted as they rode the carriage into town. Beside her, Albert reached out and laid a hand gently over hers.

"It will be all right," he murmured.

Eleanor nodded, but she was less certain than her husband. What if Henry did not wish to be taken in? Or worse—what if he found a happy home at Cartwright Manor, only to be taken away when his father was located? The poor child had suffered enough heartache.

As had she.

Could her heart survive being broken in that way? She knew the pain of longing, the grief of blessings not realized. Month after month, year after year, she forced the pieces of her heart together again, stitching them together with hope and faith. But the death of baby James made her realize the acuteness of the pain Mrs. Manwill must have suffered. It would not be the same thing, of course. But could Eleanor open her heart to love Henry as her own? Was she willing to risk the heartache for a child she may not keep?

They pulled up in front of the church before Eleanor had made her decision. Smiling his encouragement, Albert stepped out of the carriage and turned to help her down as well. Her hand trembled as she rested it in his, and he placed it firmly in the crook of his arm as they started forward. Never before had the short walk up to the parsonage caused her so much anxiety.

Their knock was answered almost immediately by the Lewises' maid, who curtsied. "Good day, Mrs. Cartwright. Mr. Cartwright. Mrs. Lewis is in the parlor," she said, leading the way.

A tray of tea and refreshments were waiting for them, as well as Mrs. Lewis and Henry Manwill. They were sitting beside one another on the small sofa, with a book laid out between them. Mrs. Lewis looked up at their entrance.

"Here they are!" she cried, rising with a smile. "I knew they would not disappoint us."

The women embraced. "He was worried you would not come," Mrs. Lewis murmured in Eleanor's ear.

Guilt pierced Eleanor's heart, for they were later than expected. She had lingered at the Bryants' and again at the Murdochs', dreading the meeting here. But she forced a smile and ducked her head in apology.

Albert was crouched over, inspecting the book which Henry held out to him.

"Mrs. Lewis is teaching me my letters," he said proudly. "This is H, for Henry."

"Very good. My name is Albert, and that begins with an A. Do you know which letter that is?"

Solemnly the little boy turned back a few pages and pointed to a large letter A, which was accompanied by a picture of an apple.

"Smart lad!" Albert said, tousling the boy's hair and standing upright. He smiled encouragingly at Eleanor, who took a step forward.

"Hello, Henry."

"Hello."

"We have come to take you home with us. Would you like that?"

Henry glanced at Mrs. Lewis, who smiled and nodded. "To live with you?" he asked.

"Yes. We live south of town, at Cartwright Manor."

"It is a great estate, almost like a castle," Albert chimed in.

"A castle?" Henry repeated, perking up.

"Yes. With stone walls and floors and long, narrow windows."

"Are there any ghosts there?"

"No," Eleanor broke in quickly. "No ghosts at all." She shot Albert a look, and he shrugged.

"Good. I don't like ghosts," Henry said. "Angels are nice, but not ghosts."

"Have you ever met a ghost?" Albert asked.

"No."

"How about an angel?"

Henry's eyes darted to Eleanor, who flushed. "Yes," he murmured, looking down. "Mama is an angel now. So's baby James. I miss them."

Eleanor crouched down to look into his face. "I am sure they miss you a great deal as well."

She reached out with her handkerchief before he could wipe his nose on his sleeve. Mrs. Lewis sat down beside him again.

"I find that when I am feeling sad, a cup of tea and a biscuit go a long way to helping me feel better. Would you not agree, Mrs. Cartwright?"

"Indeed, Mrs. Lewis."

"I am feeling a bit peckish myself," Albert said, sniffing the air. "Is that lemon cake I smell, Mrs. Lewis?"

"With almond icing," she said, smiling. "Your favorite."

Mrs. Lewis went to see about the cake, while Eleanor helped Henry dry his face and blow his nose. He looked up at her over the handkerchief.

"I don't suppose you are an angel," he said matter-of-factly. "But you're still the prettiest lady I've ever seen."

Eleanor's smile wavered, and her heart trembled. She must guard herself if she were to survive his presence in her life.

"Thank you," she said. "Has Mrs. Lewis explained things to you?"

He nodded.

"Good. We are happy to share our home with you for as long as you have need of it."

"Are there any children to play with?" he asked eagerly.

Slivers of pain shot through her, and Eleanor quickly stood. Albert was there, reaching for her. He pressed his hand against her back, ensuring her of his presence, but he looked down at the boy.

"No children, but plenty of rooms to explore and a whole forest outside your window."

Henry's blue eyes brightened. "Like Sherwood forest?"

Albert laughed. "Much like it. Though our woods are not infested with outlaws."

Eleanor had composed herself by the time Mrs. Lewis arrived with the cake, and they all sat down to a delightful repast. She watched Henry throughout the meal, noting that his appetite was good but his manners were quite ill. It steadied her, and she realized that here was something she could do. Taking the boy into their home to teach and train him was acceptable. She would be kind to him, of course. And gentle, as was her nature. But admitting him into her home did not mean she had to admit him into her heart. It was too fragile at present to consider allowing his residence there, temporary as it might be.

When the refreshments had been consumed, Eleanor and Albert stood. "We must take our leave now," she said to Mrs. Lewis. Then, reaching out her hand, she added, "Come, Henry. Let us take you home."

The boy hopped down from his seat, taking her hand. As he did so, an electric current seemed to pass up Eleanor's arm and directly into her heart. It surprised her so that she nearly let go of him. Instead, she took a deep breath.

"His things are packed and waiting," Mrs. Lewis said.

Eleanor nodded while Albert went to collect his trunk. Mrs. Lewis followed them to the door.

"Be very good for Mr. and Mrs. Cartwright, now," she said to Henry. "I will come visit you, and you will see me at church."

The little boy waved to her and climbed into the carriage, followed by Eleanor and then Albert, who shut the door behind him.

The drive to Cartwright Manor was an interesting one. Though Eleanor would have been content to let it pass in silence, Henry kept up a steady stream of dialogue from the moment they were off.

"Is it far to your home?" he asked.

"Not very. Only a few miles," she said.

"Do you have horses?"

"Yes."

"I like horses. But we don't have any. Will you teach me to ride a horse?"

"Perhaps."

"I've never been this way before," Henry said, leaning forward to look out the window. "Where are the woods?"

"We shall pass through a portion of them, but the majority lie on the other side of the manor."

"Why do you call it a manor? I thought you lived in a castle?"

Eleanor looked helplessly to Albert, who was shaking with silent laughter. "A manor is another word for a grand house," she said.

"I did not say it was a castle," Albert added. "Only that it was *like* a castle."

"Oh."

They arrived home without much incident, and soon Henry was settled in a makeshift nursery on the second floor, with one of the housemaids employed as a temporary nurse. When Albert asked whether he should send out inquiries for a suitable candidate to fill the position, Eleanor dismissed his concerns.

"He shan't be with us for long," she insisted, "and I would rather not employ someone whom we may very likely have to release in a few weeks' time."

Albert frowned, but did not press the matter.

Chapter 11

"The poor child!" Beatrice lamented. "Orphaned at such a young age."

Henry had been with the Cartwrights for three days when the Eves came to call. Henry and Michael took to one another immediately, and spent the afternoon racing through the house, stealing biscuits from the kitchen and looking for secret passageways, before being once again wrestled into the nursery by their nursemaids.

"He is not an orphan," Eleanor said mildly, pouring her sister-in-law a cup of tea. "Albert means to ask his solicitor to help locate Mr. Manwill."

They were gathered in one of the smaller drawing rooms, talking over the events of the last week. The boys had been allowed to join them, on the condition that they played quietly in a corner with a toy that Michael brought. Cecelia was asleep in her mother's arms.

"Will you request guardianship of the boy?" Nathan asked, addressing Albert.

Eleanor stiffened.

"At present, our concern is simply in locating Mr. Manwill," Albert said, glancing at his wife. "He has not been seen in over a year, and we have no idea where he might be found."

"What will you do if you cannot find him?" Beatrice asked, glancing at the two boys—one with ginger curls like her husband, the other with a dark, shaggy mop.

"It has not yet been decided, should that be the case," Albert said. "The Lewises asked if we would be willing to take him in for the time being, and we are happy to oblige."

Eleanor finished pouring the tea and handed the last cup to her brother. "How do *you* feel about the arrangements, Nora?" he asked in a low voice. She forced herself to smile.

"I am happy to help," she said. "Henry is a sweet boy, but he has much to learn. There is a great deal I plan to teach him while he is with us. I do not think it will be for long, and I wish to make the most of it."

Nathaniel's eyebrows shot up. "Not long? Have you some inside information about his father's whereabouts?"

"No, but I am sure Albert will find him," she said smoothly, picking up her own cup and saucer.

"But—"

"Albert will find him."

She smiled tightly at her brother and went to sit beside her husband. Albert raised an eyebrow at her, but she shook her head.

"Well, at least the weather is warming up," Beatrice was

saying. "Perhaps this dreadful epidemic will be over before long. Two of our own servants have taken ill, and I banished them from the house until they are well again."

"The weather may be warming up, but it presents us with another dilemma. Eves, have your fields flooded as well?" Albert asked.

"A portion of them, though not terribly."

The men continued to talk of the weather, while the women turned their attention to the children.

"He seems healthy enough," Beatrice remarked, looking at Henry. "Did you not say that he was ill?"

"He *was* ill. Before his mother and brother died," Eleanor replied, keeping her voice low. "He did not suffer long, however. He seems to have a strong constitution."

"That is lucky for him, and though his poor mother is no longer with us, surely it was a comfort to her during her life. You cannot imagine the agonies a mother feels over the well-being of her children, Nora."

Eleanor did her best to deflect the barb. "I am sure your concern for the health of your children is very great."

"Oh, indeed it is. I worry so over them, Nora, you have no idea." She glanced at Henry again, then back to Eleanor. "Though, perhaps, if Mr. Manwill cannot be found…"

She looked at Eleanor expectantly, but Cecelia chose precisely that moment to awake, and Beatrice's attentions were immediately drawn to her daughter. Eleanor could have kissed her niece for her impeccable timing.

Far from waking up rested and happy, Cecelia soon began fussing and simply would not stop. Beatrice handed her over to

Eleanor in exasperation, but she even squirmed in Eleanor's arms. She cried if she was put down, and whimpered when anyone held her. No toy or treat could solace her, and after twenty minutes of her fussing, Beatrice looked helplessly at Eleanor.

"She is not usually so irritable," she said, trying again to comfort her crying daughter.

"Is she still tired, perhaps?"

"I suppose she could be, though she did just have a nap."

Eleanor examined her niece, who was writhing in her mother's arms. Her color was good and she did not feel warm. "It might be nothing—she may be tired or overstimulated. But perhaps you ought to take her home for some rest."

"I suppose you are right," Beatrice sighed. "Though I had hoped to stay for a nice long visit. It is terribly lonely at the Park."

"Come again tomorrow, if Cece is feeling better."

Beatrice smiled. "Thank you, that is most kind. Michael," she called over her shoulder, "gather your things, it is time to be going home."

Michael scrambled to his feet, and Henry did the same. "Mother, mother!" Michael cried, shouting to be heard over Cecelia's crying. "Can Henry come over to our house? He's going to be my cousin. He said—"

"Perhaps another time," Eleanor broke in. "Henry, say goodbye to our guests."

The boys mumbled their goodbyes as Beatrice and Nathaniel took their leave. Cecelia was wailing, certain to let everyone know how unhappy she was. The Eves did not linger, and soon the house was quiet once more.

"Henry, let us go back to the nursery. It is time for your tea," Eleanor said.

"Will you stay with me?" he asked, his eyes bright with anticipation.

"If you'd like. And if you promise to mind your manners."

"I would like. Very much. But why must I constantly mind my manners? I've got them, haven't I? They aren't going anywhere, are they?"

Albert hid his laugh behind a cough, while Eleanor escorted their young charge out of the room, hiding her smile behind yet another explanation.

"If the warm weather holds," Albert said at dinner the next day, "I should like to travel into Norwich to see Mr. Broderick."

"Will you be gone long?"

"No more than a day or two. I do not plan to stay for the search, only to request his help in locating Mr. Manwill, and see that he has the means to begin."

The door to the dining room opened, and Pritchett entered with Hannah, the girl now employed in looking after Henry.

"Forgive me, mistress, but you are wanted in the nursery," the butler said, bowing low.

Eleanor sighed. "I told Henry when I left that I was going to dinner and would not see him again until bedtime."

"I've told him that, mistress, but he will not listen!" Hannah said, wringing her hands. "He's climbed into the wardrobe and refuses to come out until I fetch you."

Eleanor pressed her lips into a thin line, but Albert spoke up. "Perhaps he will come out if I have a word with him," he said, getting to his feet.

"Albert—"

"I shall only be a moment."

Albert followed Hannah upstairs to the nursery. Muffled thumps were coming from the wardrobe in the corner.

"I've tried everything I can think of to coax him out," the poor girl said. "But he won't budge!"

Albert smiled. "I think I have something that will do the trick. Please wait for me in the hallway, I shan't be long."

Once the door shut behind her, Albert took off his jacket. He loosened his cravat and rolled up his shirtsleeves. Turning to face the wardrobe, he put his hands on his hips.

"All right in there," he bellowed. "I heard there was a dragon in my house and I am here to say you are most unwelcome! I shall give you to the count of three before I come in after you. One…"

Silence.

"Two…"

There was a muffled yell and a loud thump inside the wardrobe.

"Three!" Albert threw open the doors of the wardrobe, revealing a tousled pile of linens with a little boy's head sticking out of it. Henry gasped.

"I'm not a dragon!" he cried. "I'm only Henry!"

Albert eyed the boy suspiciously. "Henry, eh? You do not look like Henry to me. He is a good little boy, who never climbs into wardrobes after dragons."

Henry's cheeks flushed.

"Come on then, out you come."

Albert helped Henry extricate himself from the contents of the closet and pulled him out. He set the lad down and crouched to look into his eyes.

"Hm, I guess you are Henry," he said. "But what were you doing in the wardrobe?"

"I was hoping Mrs. Cartwright would come," he said, looking at his feet.

Albert's look softened. "Mrs. Cartwright is having dinner. Did she not tell you as much?"

"Yes," came the mumbled reply.

"Have you had your dinner?" Albert asked.

Henry looked to the empty table. "No. Hannah said I couldn't have my dinner until I came out of the wardrobe."

"Well, you are out now. Shall I tell her to bring it up for you?"

"Will you eat it with me?" Henry's voice was hopeful.

"No—I am having dinner with Mrs. Cartwright."

"Oh." The boy's face fell. "I wish I had someone to have dinner with."

"Does not your nurse have dinner with you?"

"Yes, but she doesn't count," Henry said. "At home, I used to have dinner with my mother. That is why I wanted Mrs. Cartwright to come. She's like my mother now, isn't she?"

Albert hesitated.

"I miss having a mother," Henry said, digging his toe into the rug. "I wish Mrs. Cartwright would be my mother now."

Eleanor had finished her meal but was still at the table when Albert returned. "Well?" she asked.

"He is out of the wardrobe, and is eating his dinner now. He looks forward to seeing you at bedtime, as promised."

Eleanor raised her brow but said nothing, and Albert took his seat and resumed eating. After only a few bites, he laid his fork down and pushed away from the table. "Nora," he asked, turning to face his wife. "What if decided to keep Henry ourselves, instead of looking for Mr. Manwill."

"Keep him! Albert! Mr. Manwill is his father. We cannot keep the boy from him."

"I know that," Albert said, frowning. "But the man obviously cares very little for what happens to his family. Who is to say that he would not mind another raising his son as their own?"

"It is not our place to decide for him," she said stiffly.

"Of course not. I am merely suggesting that instead of looking for him, we let him find us, when and if he so chooses."

Eleanor looked so sharply at him, that Albert flinched. "Nora," he said. "Henry needs a stable home. He needs a family."

Eleanor's face was grave. "No, Albert," she said quietly, rising from the table. "Henry has a father. Mr. Manwill is his father."

Albert's look softened. "It is not a father that Henry needs so much as a mother, Nora."

She said nothing.

"Do you know what he said to me upstairs just now? He told me that he missed having a mother. That he wished *you* were his mother."

The barriers around Eleanor's heart trembled.

"Even if he were to go and live with his father," Albert

continued, "he still would not have a mother."

"He might, someday," Eleanor said curtly.

"Perhaps, but—"

"Is Mr. Broderick expecting you?" she asked suddenly.

Albert sighed. "Yes, but—"

"Good. Then you shall leave in the morning as planned. The sooner we find Henry's father, the sooner he will have another home," she said, wrapping her arms around herself. "And that is what is best."

Chapter 12

The collective prayers of the entire community finally came to fruition, and the weather began to warm. Thin winter sunshine, weak though it was, forced its way through the ever-present clouds, warming the hearts and homes of Littleton. The Kirks finally recovered from pneumonia, and the Bryants were on the mend as well. For the first time in weeks, Eleanor's heart felt light.

Albert had asked that the carriage be ready first thing after breakfast. He hoped to get to Norwich in time to meet with his solicitor, Mr. Broderick, before business closed for the day.

"With any luck, I shall be home tomorrow," he said, kissing Eleanor goodbye.

"It will be lonely here without you," she said.

"Not too lonely, I hope. Your brother is just down the road, and Henry is here." He smiled, but Eleanor only sighed, shaking her head.

When the carriage had disappeared down the lane, Eleanor turned back into the house and made her way to the nursery. Stopping before the door, she took a deep breath, ensuring that her heart was safely ensconced within its walls.

Henry's face lit up as she came into the room. "You came back!" he cried, running at her.

"I told you I would," she said mildly. "But do not squeeze me so, Henry, or you shall muss my dress."

Henry stepped back, and Eleanor took another breath. The truth was, she hardly cared whether her clothing was creased or not. But whenever Henry embraced her, the fetters around her heart threatened to break. The longer he remained with them, the more attached she grew, and the harder it was to force her heart to be still.

"Now, where were we?" she said brightly, sitting down at the table. Henry climbed onto the chair next to her and pointed at the open book before them.

"We were on the letter L," he said. "L is for Lion."

"Very good. That is a picture of a lion. What else begins with the *l* sound?"

"Lollipop!" he cried. Eleanor smiled.

"Yes, lollipop has two *l* sounds. Anything else?"

Henry frowned, thinking. "Licorice!" he said after a moment.

Eleanor laughed. "You have a bit of a sweet tooth, I think." She turned the page in the book. "Do you know what comes after L?"

Henry sang quietly to himself for a moment before calling out, "M! M comes after L."

"Yes, it does. This is the letter M." She pointed to the large block letter on the page. "Can you tell what this picture is?"

Henry looked at the drawing carefully. "Is it a rat?"

"It is similar. What is similar to a rat that begins with *m*?"

"*M*... *m*... mouse!" he cried triumphantly.

"Very good! Now, what else can you think of that starts with the letter M?"

"Milk! I like milk with my biscuits."

"So do I," Eleanor said. "Would you like some now?"

"Yes, please."

Eleanor smiled. She was happy to see that one lesson, at least, had been learned. The last two days had been spent teaching Henry to say *please* and *thank you* appropriately, and she rejoiced in her success.

"I know another word that starts with *m*," he said around a mouthful of cookie.

"We do not speak when there is food in our mouths, Henry."

"Sorry," he mumbled. She shot him a stern look, and he ducked his head. Swallowing, he said, "Want to hear my word?"

Before she could answer, he blurted out, "*Mother*. Mother begins with M." His blue eyes looked up into hers, full of pain and longing.

Eleanor stood abruptly, just as the door opened and her breathless housekeeper stepped in, followed by Nathaniel.

"Mr. Eves to see you, m—"

"I don't need an introduction!" Nathaniel growled. "Nora, we need you."

"Why, what has happened?"

"Cecelia is ill. We think it might be influenza."

Eleanor gasped. "Are you sure?"

Her brother nodded. "She's hot as Hades and so mucked up she can hardly breathe."

"I shall come at once. How is Beatrice?"

Nathaniel shook his head. "Barely keeping it together."

"And Michael?"

"Safely confined to the nursery. No sign of illness in him yet."

Eleanor breathed a sigh of relief as she stepped towards the door.

"Wait!"

Eleanor turned around as Henry came running up to her. She held out her hand.

"Our lesson will have to wait, Henry."

"Please, don't go, Mrs. Cartwright," he said, his little voice unsteady. "Mr. Cartwright left... if you leave too, I'll be all alone."

"Albert is gone?" Nathaniel asked.

"He left for business in Norwich."

"Please, Mrs. Cartwright." Henry started to cry, but Eleanor would not have it. She crouched down and looked squarely into his face. She was not smiling.

"Henry, you are not alone. Hannah is here, and there is a whole houseful of servants besides," she said, her voice tight.

"But... *you* won't be here."

Eleanor's heart fluttered, but she clamped it down tightly. "I am sorry," she said, getting to her feet. "I must go."

She turned on her heel and strode from the room, with Nathaniel following right behind. The only indication that she heard Henry's wails was the tightness in her jaw.

"Nora," Nathaniel said, his voice less urgent. "If you need to stay…"

"Henry will be fine. Cecelia needs me."

Nathaniel said no more until they reached the entrance hall. "The road is mostly dry. You shouldn't have trouble getting the carriage through. I must find Mrs. Jones."

Eleanor nodded. "If she is not at home, try the Granthams. Or the Kirks."

Thanking her, Nathaniel strode out the front door. Eleanor sent word to have the carriage readied immediately.

The carriage ride to Edgewood Park took less than a half hour, but it was agony for Eleanor. Would Cecelia be all right? Was she terribly ill? She was only a few months younger than the Manwill baby… but Eleanor forced the thought from her mind. Cecelia would not die. She could not die.

Eleanor pressed her hands to her stomach, feeling the thrum of her heart. She looked through the windows, craning her neck, willing the trees to pass more quickly. Where was the house? Should they not be there by now? Closing her eyes she offered a silent prayer, panic building in her breast like the water behind a dam.

At last they turned down the familiar drive, and her heart jumped into her throat. She was out of the carriage and running up the steps before the horses had fully stopped.

The servants were expecting her, for which she was glad. She picked up her skirts and followed a housemaid quickly up the stairs, anxiety knotting her stomach. She was directed to a guest room on the second floor, which had been hastily converted into a hospital room for the sick child.

The room was well lit, and quite warm from the fire roaring in the hearth. Beatrice stood in the middle of the room, cradling her daughter. She turned at Eleanor's entrance, her pretty face pinched with worry, but her expression melted away in surprise upon seeing her.

"Eleanor! What are you doing here? I sent Nathan to find Mrs. Jones…"

"He stopped by the manor on his way into town. I directed him to where Mrs. Jones might be," Eleanor said, crossing the room to her sister-in-law. "How is she?"

Beatrice sighed. "She has finally fallen asleep. The poor thing is exhausted."

Eleanor peeked over her sister-in-law's shoulder at her sleeping niece. Cecelia's eyes were closed. Two bright spots, one on each cheek, looked as if they were painted on with rouge. Her breathing was somewhat labored, but slow and steady.

"When did it begin?"

"Late last night. Nurse MacDowell put the children to bed without much trouble, but she awakened me before dawn, concerned about Cece. Of course, I arose at once and went to the nursery, where I found her much like this."

"The room is warm. Is she coughing at all?"

"Only a bit."

Eleanor gently brushed her niece's cheek, pulling her hand back quickly. "Good heavens! She is on fire!"

Beatrice groaned. "We have been trying to keep her cool, but if we undress her anymore she begins to shake and tremble quite violently."

Eleanor walked over to the cradle on the other side of the

room. She smoothed out the blankets, ensuring that it was soft and comfortable. "Would you like to lay her down?"

Beatrice shook her head. "I am afraid to move her, lest she awaken."

Reaching out her arms, Eleanor smiled. "Would you like me to hold her, then? I know how it can tire your arms, carrying her for so long."

"Thank you, but I would rather wait until Mrs. Jones is here."

Letting her arms drop, Eleanor seated herself beside the cradle and waited. After several minutes, Beatrice walked slowly to the settee across from Eleanor and gingerly sat down. Cecelia stirred, but in a moment she calmed, and her mother released a breath.

The minutes passed slowly, each one more anxious than the last. Eleanor's hands were clasped so tightly in her lap that her knuckles were white. She watched Cece in silence, waiting.

At last, voices were heard in the hallway outside. Eleanor stood as the door opened and Nathaniel, followed by Henrietta Jones, strode into the room. Beatrice looked up, and Nathaniel quickly crossed the room to kneel beside his wife.

"How is she?" he asked, his voice barely a whisper.

"There has been no improvement," Beatrice said.

"Mr. Eves apprised me of her condition on the drive over," Mrs. Jones said, removing her wraps. "Is she still quite warm?"

"Exceedingly so," Beatrice answered.

Without another word, the old midwife plucked the babe from her mother's arms. Beatrice cried out in protest, but Mrs. Jones merely shook her head.

"I need her awake. She'll sleep again soon enough."

Laying the now-wailing child in the little crib, she pulled the

83

blankets away from her body and began to undress her. Beatrice hovered nervously at Mrs. Jones's shoulder.

Mrs. Jones murmured quietly to herself as she performed her examination, her patient crying and writhing in displeasure. "Far too hot, but no sign of a rash. Good." She carefully grasped Cecelia's cheeks and peered into her mouth. Next, she rolled her over and checked her back, placing an ear against her pink skin and listening intently. At last she picked her up and handed her back to Beatrice, who immediately began to rock and shush her daughter.

"Well?" Nathaniel and Eleanor said in unison.

" 'Tis influenza, all right. She's in for a rough few weeks, but her lungs are clear for now, and that is a good sign."

"Is there anything we can do?" Beatrice asked.

"Keep her covered, but use a cold compress on her head—we don't want her getting brain fever. Make sure she eats, and call me at once if her breathing gets any more labored."

Beatrice nodded, and both she and Nathaniel bent over their daughter, speaking to her quietly and attempting to lull her back to sleep. Eleanor crossed over to Mrs. Jones.

"Will she be all right?" she asked, keeping her voice low. The midwife nodded.

"Aye. 'Tis not a bad case, and she looks healthy enough."

"But she is only ten months old." Eleanor bit her lip. "The Manwill baby was hardly older than that."

Mrs. Jones's look softened. "Don't fret now, Mrs. Cartwright. She'll pull through."

Eleanor could only nod, hoping it was true.

Chapter 13

Eleanor stayed at her brother's house for the rest of the day. She hovered in the nursery, anxious to be of use, doing many tasks for which a servant would normally have been called upon to perform. She stoked the fire, changed the linens, went to the kitchen and brought back tea—anything to relieve her nervous energy. Mrs. Jones seemed confident that Cece would recover, but Eleanor knew far too well how quickly an illness can turn, especially in little ones.

The curtains had been drawn and the lamps lit when Eleanor stood from her chair and stretched her neck. She had been gone all day, and for a moment, a sliver of guilt pierced her heart as she thought of Henry all alone at Cartwright Manor. She shook her head quickly, dispelling the image and telling her mind—and her heart—that Henry was perfectly well at home. He did not need her there. She was needed here.

Nathaniel was dozing in a chair by the window, the lines of stress and worry temporarily erased from his forehead. Eleanor looked over at her niece, now sleeping quietly in her crib, and then at her sister-in-law, who was staring absently into the fire. Eleanor went quietly over to her.

"Go get some rest, Beatrice," Eleanor said. "I can sit with her."

"Thank you, but I cannot possibly leave little Cece," Beatrice said, looking up at her with a slight frown. Eleanor smiled at her gently.

"You are exhausted, my dear sister. You need your rest."

"And Cece needs her mother," she said firmly, rising from her place. Nathaniel huffed in his sleep, and both women looked anxiously towards the crib, but Cecelia did not stir. "I know you mean well," Beatrice continued, more gently, "but you do not understand how it feels to see your child so helpless and ill. No," she shook her head emphatically, "there will be no rest for me. Not until my daughter is well."

She smiled sadly at Eleanor. "We shall be all right. Thank you for your concern, but you should go home now. Your own family needs you."

"Albert is in Norwich," Eleanor murmured.

"But Henry is there."

Eleanor knew that her sister-in-law did not know, could not understand, the reason for the distance Eleanor felt compelled to keep between herself and Henry. But she smiled weakly and nodded.

"Of course. I shall see myself out."

Eleanor mulled over Beatrice's words on the way back to the

manor. They did not sit well, and she wondered why it rankled her so. *Cece needs her mother*, she'd said. Well, of course she did. But did it follow that she needed no one else? Eleanor knew the love she had for her niece and nephew could not compare to the love their parents had for them, but were they only capable of accepting love from their mother and father? The thought was absurd.

By the time she returned home, Eleanor's head was aching. Whether it was from the strain to her nerves or the jostling from the carriage, she knew not. All she knew was that her head hurt abominably, and she wanted nothing more than to lie down and rest.

"Has everything been well here today?" she asked Mrs. Winthrop, removing her gloves.

The housekeeper sighed. "Not entirely, mistress."

"Oh?"

"Master Henry had a rough day of it. Crying and wailing like I never heard before. Said he didn't want to be alone."

Guilt pricked at Eleanor's heart. "Is he sleeping now?"

"Yes, mistress. Cried himself to sleep after refusing his supper."

Eleanor rubbed her temple, trying to push off the guilt she knew she deserved to feel. Well, there was nothing for it now. Henry was asleep, and nothing could be said or done until morning. She sighed.

"Thank you, Mrs. Winthrop. That will be all."

A knock on Eleanor's bedroom door pulled her from sleep. She rubbed her eyes and sat up, trying to make sense of her surroundings.

The knocking grew more insistent.

Climbing out of bed, Eleanor went to the door and opened it a crack.

"Begging your pardon, mistress, but Master Henry won't stop crying. I've tried everything to comfort him but all he does is wail."

Hannah's desperate eyes looked up at Eleanor, who sighed.

"I shall be right down."

Tying a robe about her and throwing a shawl over her shoulders, Eleanor took up a candle and walked swiftly down the corridor towards the main staircase. Shadows morphed and mutated against the high stone walls as she went, the light from the candle illuminating tapestries and portraits of long-dead residents, only to plunge them once more into darkness as she strode past.

She heard Henry's cries before she even reached the landing. His sobs were punctuated with cries for… she could not make out what. Stopping before the nursery door, she took a deep breath. Concern for her niece and fatigue served to weaken her restraint, and she paused a moment to tighten the armor over her heart.

The room was illuminated by several candles, and a small fire had been lit in the grate. The housemaid-turned-nurse was sitting on the edge of the bed next to Henry, who was swallowing his sobs as Eleanor entered the room. Hannah looked up at her entrance.

"He keeps calling for his mum. I don't know what to do."

"Let me stay with him for a time, while you fetch us some tea, if you please."

Relief flooded the young woman's face and she swiftly left the room, leaving Eleanor staring at Henry's tear-streaked face. He stared gloomily back at her.

"I want my mum," he said, a fresh wave of tears starting.

Eleanor sat down beside him. "I am sorry, dear. I know you miss her."

"I want my mum," he said again.

A different sort of pain coursed through Eleanor as she watched him. Pain from far away memories, following the death of her own mother. She had not been much older than Henry was now.

It is not a father that Henry needs so much as a mother, Albert had said. Just like Cece needed her mother. Just as Eleanor had needed her mother—oh, so many times!—throughout her life. But Eleanor's mother died giving birth to Nathaniel, and though her father had been loving and attentive, nothing he did could repair the hole that was left in Eleanor's heart after her mother's death.

Henry was sobbing, his knees drawn up to his chest, his arms wrapped around them. Eleanor reached a hand out and gently stroked his hair, feeling the coarseness beneath her fingertips for the first time. She felt her heart reaching out to him, desperately trying to break free from the walls she had built around it. Her head was playing at tug-of-war, calling it back, citing all the reasons she should remain aloof. In the midst of the turmoil, Albert's words came back to her.

Perhaps God has answered our prayers in another way.

But could there be another way? All her life, Eleanor had

dreamed of being a mother. When it appeared she would not marry, she had tucked that dream away, resigned to cheer and bless the lives of those around her instead. But then Albert came into her life, and her dream of motherhood resurfaced, rendered even more brilliant from the test of time. After they married, she watched, and waited.

And waited.

And waited.

In her mind, the dream of motherhood included a growing belly and a precious infant, hers to love and dote upon from the very moment of existence. She had never imagined, never even considered, that God may have had a different sort of motherhood in mind.

Another way.

Tears pricked her eyes, and as they fell her defenses crumbled. She pulled the boy into her arms, holding him close. He responded to her touch immediately, and soon they were weeping together, holding on to one another for comfort and strength.

They remained that way for a long time, until the door opened and Hannah returned with a tray of tea. Eleanor dried her eyes, and tenderly dried Henry's as well.

"There now, it is all right. I am here, and you are safe."

Henry sniffed. "I miss my mum," he said again. "But I'm glad I have you."

Eleanor kissed the top of his head, feeling the gaps in her heart filling with love. "I am glad I have you too, Henry."

Chapter 14

Albert returned from Norwich two days later, after having done all he could to begin the search for Mr. Manwill. He was not overly concerned that it might be months or even years before Mr. Manwill could be located, but he was concerned about the toll a prolonged search might take on Eleanor. He hoped her heart would soften somewhat towards their young charge.

Pritchett greeted him with a strange smile upon his entering the house.

"Where is Eleanor?" Albert asked.

His butler bowed. "I believe she is in the library, with Master Henry."

That surprised him. Why was Henry not in the nursery? He nodded his thanks and took himself down the hall, the sharp clack of his cane on the stone floors marking his approach. He opened the library door without knocking, and saw his wife seated beside

Henry on the couch, their heads so close together that Eleanor's warm brown locks mingled with Henry's tousled black ones. They looked up at his entrance.

"Papa!" Henry cried, jumping down from the sofa. Albert started.

"Henry," Eleanor called, and Henry turned back. "Remember, you must ask Mr. Cartwright if you may call him that before you actually begin doing so."

"Oh, yes. Sorry." Henry grinned up at Albert. "Mr. Cartwright? May I call you Papa? Mrs. Cartwright said that I may call her Mama now, and it would be jolly fun if I could have a Papa, too."

Albert looked up into Eleanor's laughing eyes, incredulous. He cleared his throat.

"Well now," he said, "I would prefer to be addressed as Sir Gallant the Dragonslayer, but I suppose Papa will do."

Henry let out a whoop and began dancing around the room, and after several failed attempts to calm him down Eleanor gave up. She stood and walked to her husband's side, a sheepish look on her face.

"You were right," she said, tipping her head back. Albert brushed his lips against hers, taking her into his arms.

"I am glad to be right on occasion," he said. "But to what in particular are you referring?"

"Him," she said, nodding at Henry, who was still dancing around the room. "Me. God. All of it. You were right."

"What happened?"

Eleanor smiled, and Albert's breath caught in his chest. It was the first genuine smile he had seen on her face in many, many years. She took his hand.

"Come," she said, leading him to the sofa. "I shall tell you all about it."

Two weeks had passed since Albert's return, and at last spring came to their little corner of England. Those whose health had been affected by the epidemic cheered the sunny skies, but not before the influenza had claimed a final victim. After a valiant effort and several close calls, young Matthew Whitman finally succumbed to pneumonia. The town was heartbroken at another loss from their midst, and Eleanor wept as he was laid to rest in the little graveyard behind the church.

But her heavy heart did not last long. She awoke one morning to find that the dark, barren landscape was covered in a filmy green haze, barely perceptible if one looked for its source, but omnipresent as one gazed out upon the view. It lifted her heart and cheered her considerably.

Since Albert's return, Eleanor had spent most of her time at home, becoming better acquainted with Henry. After her sister-in-law's kind but clear dismissal, she had been hesitant to call upon her brother, trusting that if Cece grew worse they would send for her at once. But today she knew she must pay Beatrice a visit, and her stomach turned uncomfortably at the thought.

Eleanor waited in the drawing room of her childhood home for what seemed like an eternity. She twisted her hands in her lap, memorizing the pattern of carpet under her feet as she waited for her sister-in-law to join her. At last the door opened, and Beatrice entered the room.

"Sorry to keep you waiting. Cece simply will not settle down for her nap! Nurse MacDowell is with her now."

"So she is doing better now?" Eleanor asked, standing tensely in front of her chair.

"Heavens, yes! She was only truly ill for a couple days, though she still has a cough. Her fever is gone and her energy has returned. I only wish mine would as well."

She gave Eleanor a tired smile, and the ladies sat down again. "Now, Jensen said you wished to speak with me?"

"Yes, I did." Eleanor folded her hands in her lap and took a deep breath. "Beatrice, I owe you an apology."

"An apology! Why, whatever for?"

Eleanor hesitated. "I am afraid that my overly sensitive heart may have, on occasion, taken offense at your words or deeds when no offense was meant. I have, at times, harbored ill feelings towards yourself, and for that I truly apologize."

Beatrice inclined her head in acceptance.

"I also fear," Eleanor continued, "that in my anxious desire to be a mother, I may have overstepped my boundaries as an aunt at times. If my words or actions have ever given you cause to think less of your place and position, I am very sorry, and hope you will forgive me. I have been quite jealous of you, you know."

Beatrice's surprised eyes were filled with tears. "Oh, Nora," she said, reaching for her handkerchief. "You know not how long I have yearned for what you have!"

"What *I* have?" Eleanor cried.

"Indeed," Beatrice nodded, wiping her eyes. "You, whom all the children in the parish love. You, whose opinion and help are sought by everyone in town. You, who can do no wrong in your brother's eyes…"

"Oh! I cannot believe that," Eleanor said, embarrassed. "Nathan has certainly felt the brunt of my censure and criticism during his lifetime—surely he does not feel that I am wholly without fault."

"But he does," Beatrice sighed. "Whenever I have a question regarding the household or accounts, he always advises me to ask you."

"Me?"

"Yes. And when Cece was ill, and I sent him to find Mrs. Jones? He went to find you, instead. He told me initially to send for you; that you would know what to do. But I was stubborn, and jealous, and did not want you." She dropped her eyes. "I am sorry for my pettiness."

Eleanor reached out to her, and the women clasped hands. "Dear Beatrice! I suppose we both have been jealous and petty at times, but all is now forgiven."

"Yes, indeed," Beatrice said, smiling again. "Thank you, dear sister, for your kindness. I am glad that we are neighbors."

"I am glad of it, too, most particularly because I will need your help in the coming months."

"Oh?"

"Yes. You see," Eleanor flushed, "I have decided that, whether or not we are able to locate Mr. Manwill, we will treat Henry as our own while he is in our home. And as much as I care to think I know all about raising boys from my interactions with my nephew, I haven't the faintest idea what I am doing."

Beatrice laughed. "Oh, Nora!" She smiled indulgently at her.

"Welcome to motherhood. None of us have any idea what we are doing."

Epilogue

Nine months later
December 1852

"Hush now, they are coming!"

The sounds of a carriage pulling to a stop in front of the house was lost on Henry, who squirmed beside Eleanor. "Why do we have to get all dressed up for Uncle Nathan and Aunt Beatrice?" he said, making a face. "We see them every day!"

"Because today is Christmas, and that makes it special," Eleanor patiently replied. "Dear, stop pulling on your cravat, please. You shall muss it."

Albert, standing on the other side of Henry, cleared his throat. He clasped his hands behind his back and looked down at the boy, his brow raised expectantly. Henry sighed and stopped his fidgeting.

"There's a good boy," Eleanor said, smiling at her son.

"I'm only being good because Papa promised me a wooden horse if I behaved myself," he mumbled. Eleanor's eyebrows shot up as she looked to Albert, who coughed.

Suddenly the front door burst open, and Beatrice and Nathaniel Eves stood on the threshold with their two young children. "Happy Christmas!" they cried.

"Happy Christmas!" the Cartwrights chorused back. The families dissolved into laughter and smiles, while everybody spoke at once and no one heard a thing. Henry wriggled his way through the crowd of skirts and coats and boots until he was at Michael's side. "Come on," he hissed. "I've got loads of new toys to show you!"

The boys scampered off as the adults made their way into the drawing room and the melee in the entrance hall died down. It was a slow procession, as they had to accommodate Cecelia, who toddled along next to her mother.

"Nora, you've outdone yourself," Nathaniel said, looking around with admiration. Boughs of evergreen branches had been woven together into long swags, which crossed over their heads as they walked down the hall. Crimson ribbon tied in elegant bows added warmth and color to the space, and above each doorway hung clusters of mistletoe. He stopped in the entrance to the drawing room and kissed his wife.

"For luck," he said, winking at his sister.

The drawing room had been transformed into a wonderland of golden light. Dozens of candles illuminated the large, airy room, and a massive fire roared in the hearth. A Christmas tree over ten feet tall stood by the front windows, decorated with paper flowers, ribbons, and even more candles. Cecelia pointed to the tree with a chubby finger.

"Pwetty," she said.

"Where are Michael and Henry?" Beatrice asked, looking around. "I thought they came in before us."

"Probably up in the nursery," Albert said. "I expect Henry wants to show his cousin all his new treasures."

"They shall miss Christmas dinner if they do not hurry," Eleanor said, pulling a bell to call one of the servants. She sent the maid who answered her summons to bring the boys downstairs.

"Have you heard anything from Manwill?" Nathaniel asked.

"Not since he signed the papers granting us guardianship of Henry," Albert replied. "And that was months ago."

"I am glad it all turned out well," Beatrice said.

"Not so glad as we are," Eleanor replied, smiling. "Henry is the dearest boy, though he gets into his fair share of mischief."

"Little boys are made for mischief," Nathaniel said, quirking his eyebrow at his sister. She laughed.

"*You* certainly were," she said. "Father was forever punishing you for something or other you had done."

"If I remember correctly," Nathaniel drawled, "my older sister put me up to a lot of those things."

Pritchett came into the room just then, and announced that dinner was ready.

"Where are Henry and Michael?" Eleanor asked. "I sent someone to fetch them."

"Here they are," Nathaniel called, as the boys burst into the room.

"Sorry, Mother," Henry panted. "I was showing Michael my new soldiers!"

"Well, thank you for coming down," she said. "Although I hope you were not running through the halls?"

Albert laughed at the chagrin on Henry's face. "We can make allowances on Christmas day, I think," he said, and Henry grinned.

The group went in to dinner—Eleanor taking Albert's arm and the rest following behind. Albert stood at the head of the table while everyone else found their seats. Eleanor sat to his right, with Henry beside her. Her brother Nathaniel sat directly across from her, and he grinned at her as he sat down. Even little Cece, at Eleanor's insistence, was seated at the table with them. Henry's hand found Eleanor's and squeezed it underneath the table.

"This is the best Christmas ever," he whispered.

Eleanor looked around the table, tears forming in her eyes. Yes, it was indeed the best Christmas ever.

Acknowledgments

They say that raising a child takes a village, and writing a book is the same way. My gratitude goes first and foremost to my Heavenly Father, without whose daily help I would not be able to accomplish anything

To my dear husband, John. Thank you for joining me on this crazy journey. Your continual support and encouragement keep me going every day. I love you.

For my friends and fellow writers, who read, critiqued, and advised, and most especially to Sally Britton. Thank you for your kind words, helpful suggestions, and nightly chat sessions. I am so blessed to call you my friend!

Finally, to all those who read and loved Christmas at Edgewood Park. Without your comments, reviews, and emails which begged for more, this story would never have happened. Thank you for loving Eleanor and Albert as much as I do. I hope you have enjoyed their happily ever after.

About the Author

 Shaela Kay was born and raised near Seattle, Washington. She studied Theatre and English at Brigham Young University-Idaho, but left her studies in order to be a wife and a mother. When she isn't writing, you can find her quilting, crafting, or homeschooling her four children. She and her husband John live with their family in a little house along the banks of the mighty Columbia River. Visit her online at www.shaelakay.com.